SILENT PRAYER

(A Sheila Stone Suspense Thriller—Book Eight)

BLAKE PIERCE

\

Blake Pierce

Blake Pierce is the USA Today bestselling author of the RILEY PAGE mystery series, which includes seventeen books. Blake Pierce is also the author of the MACKENZIE WHITE mystery series, comprising fourteen books; of the AVERY BLACK mystery series, comprising six books; of the KERI LOCKE mystery series, comprising five books; of the MAKING OF RILEY PAIGE mystery series, comprising six books; of the KATE WISE mystery series, comprising seven books; of the CHLOE FINE psychological suspense mystery, comprising six books; of the JESSIE HUNT psychological suspense thriller series, comprising thirty-eight books (and counting); of the AU PAIR psychological suspense thriller series, comprising three books; of the ZOE PRIME mystery series, comprising six books; of the ADELE SHARP mystery series, comprising sixteen books, of the EUROPEAN VOYAGE cozy mystery series, comprising six books; of the LAURA FROST FBI suspense thriller, comprising eleven books; of the ELLA DARK FBI suspense thriller, comprising twenty-five books (and counting); of the A YEAR IN EUROPE cozy mystery series, comprising nine books, of the AVA GOLD mystery series, comprising six books; of the RACHEL GIFT mystery series, comprising fifteen books; of the VALERIE LAW mystery series, comprising nine books; of the PAIGE KING mystery series, comprising eight books; of the MAY MOORE mystery series, comprising eleven books; of the CORA SHIELDS mystery series, comprising eight books; of the NICKY LYONS mystery series, comprising eight books, of the CAMI LARK mystery series, comprising ten books; of the AMBER YOUNG mystery series, comprising eight books; of the DAISY FORTUNE mystery series, comprising five books; of the FIONA RED mystery series, comprising thirteen books; of the FAITH BOLD mystery series, comprising twenty books (and counting); of the JULIETTE HART mystery series, comprising five books; of the MORGAN CROSS mystery series, comprising thirteen books; of the FINN WRIGHT mystery series, comprising seven books; of the SHEILA STONE suspense thriller series, comprising ten books; of the RACHEL BLACKWOOD suspense thriller series, comprising eight books; of the THE GOVERNESS psychological suspense thriller series, comprising nine books (and counting); and of the new JENNA GRAVES mystery series, comprising eight books (and counting).

An avid reader and lifelong fan of the mystery and thriller genres,

Blake loves to hear from you, so please feel free to visit www.blakepierceauthor.com to learn more and stay in touch.

ISBN: 978-1-0943-8693-5

BOOKS BY BLAKE PIERCE

JENNA GRAVES SUSPENSE THRILLER
IN HER SIGHTS (Book #1)
IN HER MIND (Book #2)
IN HER GRASP (Book #3)
IN HER SHADOW (Book #4)
IN HER PRAYERS (Book #5)
IN HER BED (Book #6)
IN HER DREAMS (Book #7)
IN HER FEARS (Book #8)

THE GOVERNESS PSYCHOLOGICAL SUSPENSE
ONE LAST LIE (Book #1)
ONE LAST SMILE (Book #2)
ONE LAST BREATH (Book #3)
ONE LAST GOODBYE (Book #4)
ONE LAST SECRET (Book #5)
ONE LAST WHISPER (Book #6)
ONE LAST REGRET (Book #7)
ONE LAST NIGHT (Book #8)
ONE LAST STEP (Book #9)

RACHEL BLACKWOOD SUSPENSE THRILLER
NOT THIS WAY (Book #1)
NOT THIS TIME (Book #2)
NOT THIS CLOSE (Book #3)
NOT THIS ROAD (Book #4)
NOT THIS LATE (Book #5)
NOT THIS NIGHT (Book #6)
NOT THIS PLACE (Book #7)
NOT THIS SOON (Book #8)

SHEILA STONE SUSPENSE THRILLER
SILENT GIRL (Book #1)
SILENT TRAIL (Book #2)
SILENT NIGHT (Book #3)

SILENT HOUSE (Book #4)
SILENT SCREAM (Book #5)
SILENT PREY (Book #6)
SILENT RITUAL (Book #7)
SILENT PRAYER (Book #8)
SILENT NEIGHBOR (Book #9)
SILENT SMILE (Book #10)

FINN WRIGHT MYSTERY SERIES
WHEN YOU'RE MINE (Book #1)
WHEN YOU'RE SAFE (Book #2)
WHEN YOU'RE CLOSE (Book #3)
WHEN YOU'RE SLEEPING (Book #4)
WHEN YOU'RE SANE (Book #5)
WHEN YOU'RE SILENT (Book #6)
WHEN YOU'RE GONE (Book #7)

MORGAN CROSS MYSTERY SERIES
FOR YOU (Book #1)
FOR RAGE (Book #2)
FOR LUST (Book #3)
FOR WRATH (Book #4)
FOREVER (Book #5)
FOR US (Book #6)
FOR NOW (Book #7)
FOR ONCE (Book #8)
FOR ETERNITY (Book #9)
FORLORN (Book #10)
FOR SILENCE (Book #11)
FORBIDDEN (Book #12)
FOR FEAR (Book #13)
FORSAKEN (Book #14)

JULIETTE HART MYSTERY SERIES
NOTHING TO FEAR (Book #1)
NOTHING THERE (Book #2)
NOTHING WATCHING (Book #3)
NOTHING HIDING (Book #4)
NOTHING LEFT (Book #5)

FAITH BOLD MYSTERY SERIES
SO LONG (Book #1)
SO COLD (Book #2)
SO SCARED (Book #3)
SO NORMAL (Book #4)
SO FAR GONE (Book #5)
SO LOST (Book #6)
SO ALONE (Book #7)
SO FORGOTTEN (Book #8)
SO INSANE (Book #9)
SO SMITTEN (Book #10)
SO SIMPLE (Book #11)
SO BROKEN (Book #12)
SO CRUEL (Book #13)
SO HAUNTED (Book #14)
SO SILENT (Book #15)
SO BLEAK (Book #16)
SO HOLLOW (Book #17)
SO DARK (Book #18)
SO TWISTED (Book #19)
SO WICKED (Book #20)

FIONA RED MYSTERY SERIES
LET HER GO (Book #1)
LET HER BE (Book #2)
LET HER HOPE (Book #3)
LET HER WISH (Book #4)
LET HER LIVE (Book #5)
LET HER RUN (Book #6)
LET HER HIDE (Book #7)
LET HER BELIEVE (Book #8)
LET HER FORGET (Book #9)
LET HER TRY (Book #10)
LET HER PLAY (Book #11)
LET HER VANISH (Book #12)
LET HER FADE (Book #13)

DAISY FORTUNE MYSTERY SERIES
NEED YOU (Book #1)
CLAIM YOU (Book #2)

CRAVE YOU (Book #3)
CHOOSE YOU (Book #4)
CHASE YOU (Book #5)

AMBER YOUNG MYSTERY SERIES
ABSENT PITY (Book #1)
ABSENT REMORSE (Book #2)
ABSENT FEELING (Book #3)
ABSENT MERCY (Book #4)
ABSENT REASON (Book #5)
ABSENT SANITY (Book #6)
ABSENT LIFE (Book #7)
ABSENT HUMANITY (Book #8)

CAMI LARK MYSTERY SERIES
JUST ME (Book #1)
JUST OUTSIDE (Book #2)
JUST RIGHT (Book #3)
JUST FORGET (Book #4)
JUST ONCE (Book #5)
JUST HIDE (Book #6)
JUST NOW (Book #7)
JUST HOPE (Book #8)
JUST LEAVE (Book #9)
JUST TONIGHT (Book #10)

NICKY LYONS MYSTERY SERIES
ALL MINE (Book #1)
ALL HIS (Book #2)
ALL HE SEES (Book #3)
ALL ALONE (Book #4)
ALL FOR ONE (Book #5)
ALL HE TAKES (Book #6)
ALL FOR ME (Book #7)
ALL IN (Book #8)

CORA SHIELDS MYSTERY SERIES
UNDONE (Book #1)
UNWANTED (Book #2)
UNHINGED (Book #3)

UNSAID (Book #4)
UNGLUED (Book #5)
UNSTABLE (Book #6)
UNKNOWN (Book #7)
UNAWARE (Book #8)

MAY MOORE SUSPENSE THRILLER
NEVER RUN (Book #1)
NEVER TELL (Book #2)
NEVER LIVE (Book #3)
NEVER HIDE (Book #4)
NEVER FORGIVE (Book #5)
NEVER AGAIN (Book #6)
NEVER LOOK BACK (Book #7)
NEVER FORGET (Book #8)
NEVER LET GO (Book #9)
NEVER PRETEND (Book #10)
NEVER HESITATE (Book #11)

PAIGE KING MYSTERY SERIES
THE GIRL HE PINED (Book #1)
THE GIRL HE CHOSE (Book #2)
THE GIRL HE TOOK (Book #3)
THE GIRL HE WISHED (Book #4)
THE GIRL HE CROWNED (Book #5)
THE GIRL HE WATCHED (Book #6)
THE GIRL HE WANTED (Book #7)
THE GIRL HE CLAIMED (Book #8)

VALERIE LAW MYSTERY SERIES
NO MERCY (Book #1)
NO PITY (Book #2)
NO FEAR (Book #3)
NO SLEEP (Book #4)
NO QUARTER (Book #5)
NO CHANCE (Book #6)
NO REFUGE (Book #7)
NO GRACE (Book #8)
NO ESCAPE (Book #9)

RACHEL GIFT MYSTERY SERIES
HER LAST WISH (Book #1)
HER LAST CHANCE (Book #2)
HER LAST HOPE (Book #3)
HER LAST FEAR (Book #4)
HER LAST CHOICE (Book #5)
HER LAST BREATH (Book #6)
HER LAST MISTAKE (Book #7)
HER LAST DESIRE (Book #8)
HER LAST REGRET (Book #9)
HER LAST HOUR (Book #10)
HER LAST SHOT (Book #11)
HER LAST PRAYER (Book #12)
HER LAST LIE (Book #13)
HER LAST WHISPER (Book #14)
HER LAST SECRET (Book #15)

AVA GOLD MYSTERY SERIES
CITY OF PREY (Book #1)
CITY OF FEAR (Book #2)
CITY OF BONES (Book #3)
CITY OF GHOSTS (Book #4)
CITY OF DEATH (Book #5)
CITY OF VICE (Book #6)

A YEAR IN EUROPE
A MURDER IN PARIS (Book #1)
DEATH IN FLORENCE (Book #2)
VENGEANCE IN VIENNA (Book #3)
A FATALITY IN SPAIN (Book #4)

ELLA DARK FBI SUSPENSE THRILLER
GIRL, ALONE (Book #1)
GIRL, TAKEN (Book #2)
GIRL, HUNTED (Book #3)
GIRL, SILENCED (Book #4)
GIRL, VANISHED (Book 5)
GIRL ERASED (Book #6)
GIRL, FORSAKEN (Book #7)
GIRL, TRAPPED (Book #8)

GIRL, EXPENDABLE (Book #9)
GIRL, ESCAPED (Book #10)
GIRL, HIS (Book #11)
GIRL, LURED (Book #12)
GIRL, MISSING (Book #13)
GIRL, UNKNOWN (Book #14)
GIRL, DECEIVED (Book #15)
GIRL, FORLORN (Book #16)
GIRL, REMADE (Book #17)
GIRL, BETRAYED (Book #18)
GIRL, BOUND (Book #19)
GIRL, REFORMED (Book #20)
GIRL, REBORN (Book #21)
GIRL, HAUNTED (Book #22)
GIRL, UNSEEN (Book #23)
GIRL, SOUGHT (Book #24)
GIRL, ACCUSED (Book #25)

LAURA FROST FBI SUSPENSE THRILLER

ALREADY GONE (Book #1)
ALREADY SEEN (Book #2)
ALREADY TRAPPED (Book #3)
ALREADY MISSING (Book #4)
ALREADY DEAD (Book #5)
ALREADY TAKEN (Book #6)
ALREADY CHOSEN (Book #7)
ALREADY LOST (Book #8)
ALREADY HIS (Book #9)
ALREADY LURED (Book #10)
ALREADY COLD (Book #11)

EUROPEAN VOYAGE COZY MYSTERY SERIES

MURDER (AND BAKLAVA) (Book #1)
DEATH (AND APPLE STRUDEL) (Book #2)
CRIME (AND LAGER) (Book #3)
MISFORTUNE (AND GOUDA) (Book #4)
CALAMITY (AND A DANISH) (Book #5)
MAYHEM (AND HERRING) (Book #6)

ADELE SHARP MYSTERY SERIES

LEFT TO DIE (Book #1)
LEFT TO RUN (Book #2)
LEFT TO HIDE (Book #3)
LEFT TO KILL (Book #4)
LEFT TO MURDER (Book #5)
LEFT TO ENVY (Book #6)
LEFT TO LAPSE (Book #7)
LEFT TO VANISH (Book #8)
LEFT TO HUNT (Book #9)
LEFT TO FEAR (Book #10)
LEFT TO PREY (Book #11)
LEFT TO LURE (Book #12)
LEFT TO CRAVE (Book #13)
LEFT TO LOATHE (Book #14)
LEFT TO HARM (Book #15)
LEFT TO RUIN (Book #16)

THE AU PAIR SERIES

ALMOST GONE (Book#1)
ALMOST LOST (Book #2)
ALMOST DEAD (Book #3)

ZOE PRIME MYSTERY SERIES

FACE OF DEATH (Book#1)
FACE OF MURDER (Book #2)
FACE OF FEAR (Book #3)
FACE OF MADNESS (Book #4)
FACE OF FURY (Book #5)
FACE OF DARKNESS (Book #6)

A JESSIE HUNT PSYCHOLOGICAL SUSPENSE SERIES

THE PERFECT WIFE (Book #1)
THE PERFECT BLOCK (Book #2)
THE PERFECT HOUSE (Book #3)
THE PERFECT SMILE (Book #4)
THE PERFECT LIE (Book #5)
THE PERFECT LOOK (Book #6)
THE PERFECT AFFAIR (Book #7)
THE PERFECT ALIBI (Book #8)
THE PERFECT NEIGHBOR (Book #9)

THE PERFECT DISGUISE (Book #10)
THE PERFECT SECRET (Book #11)
THE PERFECT FAÇADE (Book #12)
THE PERFECT IMPRESSION (Book #13)
THE PERFECT DECEIT (Book #14)
THE PERFECT MISTRESS (Book #15)
THE PERFECT IMAGE (Book #16)
THE PERFECT VEIL (Book #17)
THE PERFECT INDISCRETION (Book #18)
THE PERFECT RUMOR (Book #19)
THE PERFECT COUPLE (Book #20)
THE PERFECT MURDER (Book #21)
THE PERFECT HUSBAND (Book #22)
THE PERFECT SCANDAL (Book #23)
THE PERFECT MASK (Book #24)
THE PERFECT RUSE (Book #25)
THE PERFECT VENEER (Book #26)
THE PERFECT PEOPLE (Book #27)
THE PERFECT WITNESS (Book #28)
THE PERFECT APPEARANCE (Book #29)
THE PERFECT TRAP (Book #30)
THE PERFECT EXPRESSION (Book #31)
THE PERFECT ACCOMPLICE (Book #32)
THE PERFECT SHOW (Book #33)
THE PERFECT POISE (Book #34)
THE PERFECT CROWD (Book #35)
THE PERFECT CRIME (Book #36)
THE PERFECT PREY (Book #37)
THE PERFECT BETRAYAL (Book #38)

CHLOE FINE PSYCHOLOGICAL SUSPENSE SERIES
NEXT DOOR (Book #1)
A NEIGHBOR'S LIE (Book #2)
CUL DE SAC (Book #3)
SILENT NEIGHBOR (Book #4)
HOMECOMING (Book #5)
TINTED WINDOWS (Book #6)

KATE WISE MYSTERY SERIES
IF SHE KNEW (Book #1)

IF SHE SAW (Book #2)
IF SHE RAN (Book #3)
IF SHE HID (Book #4)
IF SHE FLED (Book #5)
IF SHE FEARED (Book #6)
IF SHE HEARD (Book #7)

THE MAKING OF RILEY PAIGE SERIES
WATCHING (Book #1)
WAITING (Book #2)
LURING (Book #3)
TAKING (Book #4)
STALKING (Book #5)
KILLING (Book #6)

RILEY PAIGE MYSTERY SERIES
ONCE GONE (Book #1)
ONCE TAKEN (Book #2)
ONCE CRAVED (Book #3)
ONCE LURED (Book #4)
ONCE HUNTED (Book #5)
ONCE PINED (Book #6)
ONCE FORSAKEN (Book #7)
ONCE COLD (Book #8)
ONCE STALKED (Book #9)
ONCE LOST (Book #10)
ONCE BURIED (Book #11)
ONCE BOUND (Book #12)
ONCE TRAPPED (Book #13)
ONCE DORMANT (Book #14)
ONCE SHUNNED (Book #15)
ONCE MISSED (Book #16)
ONCE CHOSEN (Book #17)

MACKENZIE WHITE MYSTERY SERIES
BEFORE HE KILLS (Book #1)
BEFORE HE SEES (Book #2)
BEFORE HE COVETS (Book #3)
BEFORE HE TAKES (Book #4)
BEFORE HE NEEDS (Book #5)

BEFORE HE FEELS (Book #6)
BEFORE HE SINS (Book #7)
BEFORE HE HUNTS (Book #8)
BEFORE HE PREYS (Book #9)
BEFORE HE LONGS (Book #10)
BEFORE HE LAPSES (Book #11)
BEFORE HE ENVIES (Book #12)
BEFORE HE STALKS (Book #13)
BEFORE HE HARMS (Book #14)

AVERY BLACK MYSTERY SERIES
CAUSE TO KILL (Book #1)
CAUSE TO RUN (Book #2)
CAUSE TO HIDE (Book #3)
CAUSE TO FEAR (Book #4)
CAUSE TO SAVE (Book #5)
CAUSE TO DREAD (Book #6)

KERI LOCKE MYSTERY SERIES
A TRACE OF DEATH (Book #1)
A TRACE OF MURDER (Book #2)
A TRACE OF VICE (Book #3)
A TRACE OF CRIME (Book #4)
A TRACE OF HOPE (Book #5)

PROLOGUE

Laura Hastings sat in her car, engine off, staring at the imposing stone facade of St. Michael's Church. Her fingers drummed nervously on the steering wheel as she debated whether to go in.

You don't need to do this, a voice in her head said. *Nobody will ever find out.*

Yes, that was true. But *she'd* know. The weight of her secret had been pressing down on her for months, threatening to crush her under its weight, and she wasn't sure she could stand it anymore.

"You have to do this," she whispered to herself, trying to summon courage. "Don't chicken out now."

A young couple walked past her car, hand in hand, chatting with easy smiles as they followed the sidewalk. Laura envied their lightness, their apparent freedom from the burden she carried.

She glanced at her watch. Ten minutes until the scheduled confession time. It was now or never.

Taking a deep breath, Laura opened her car door and stepped out. The cool autumn air caressed her face, carrying the scent of fallen leaves. She smoothed her skirt and started toward the church, each step feeling heavier than the last.

At the base of the stone steps, Laura paused again. Her heart raced. Was she really ready to speak her shame aloud?

You'll just be telling the priest. Your secrets are safe with him—it's not like you murdered anyone.

An elderly woman exited the church, noticing Laura's hesitation. "Are you alright, dear?" she asked.

Laura forced a smile. "Yes, thank you. Just...gathering my thoughts."

The woman nodded sympathetically and continued on her way. Laura watched her go, then turned back to the church. She'd come this far. She had to see it through.

With renewed determination, she climbed the steps and pulled open the heavy wooden door. The familiar scent of incense enveloped her as she entered the hushed interior. The church was entirely empty, not another soul in sight.

Laura dipped her fingers in the holy water, crossing herself out of long-ingrained habit. She made her way down the aisle, her footsteps muffled by the thick carpet runner. The confessional loomed before her, its dark wood gleaming in the soft light.

She hesitated once more, her hand on the booth's handle. Before she could change her mind, she opened the door and slipped inside.

The small space felt even more confined than she remembered, the air thick and close. She knelt on the worn cushion, her knees protesting the familiar position.

"Bless me, Father, for I have sinned," she whispered, her voice trembling. "It's been...a long time since my last confession."

There was a moment of silence, then a gentle voice came through the latticed window. "Welcome, my child. How long has it been?"

Laura swallowed hard. "Six months, Father."

"I see," the priest said, his tone free of judgment. "What brings you here today?"

She took a deep breath, steeling herself. "I've done something terrible. Something I've been carrying for months."

"God is listening, child. Speak freely."

Laura's thoughts raced, memories flooding back. The weight of her guilt pressed down on her chest, making it hard to breathe. She began to speak, her words coming out in a rush.

"I betrayed my husband, Father. I...I had an affair."

There was a pause, heavy with unspoken questions. When the priest spoke again, his voice was carefully neutral. "Can you tell me more about what happened?"

Laura hesitated. How much should she reveal? "It was a coworker. We were working late on a project, and things...escalated. It only happened once, but..."

"But the guilt remains," the priest finished for her.

"Yes," Laura whispered. "I can barely look my husband in the eye. He doesn't know, but I feel like I'm lying to him every day."

The priest was silent for a moment. When he spoke again, there was a hint of something in his voice that Laura couldn't quite identify. Curiosity? Concern?

"It takes courage to confess such a sin," he said. "Have you considered telling your husband?"

Laura's hands clenched in her lap. "I've thought about it. But I'm afraid. What if he leaves me? What if I destroy our family over one stupid mistake?"

"These are difficult questions," the priest said softly. "But tell me, why did you choose to confess this now?"

She hadn't expected this question. Laura paused, considering. "I...I can't move forward. The guilt is eating me alive. I thought if I confessed, if I sought forgiveness..."

"You thought you could find peace," the priest finished for her.

"Yes," Laura said, relief flooding through her. He understood.

"And what would you do with this peace, if you found it?"

The question caught her off guard. "I...I'm not sure. Try to be a better wife, I suppose. Make amends, somehow."

There was another pause, longer this time. When the priest spoke again, his tone had changed subtly. "And you believe you deserve this peace? After betraying your husband's trust?"

Laura's breath caught in her throat. The priest's words were harsher than she'd expected.

"Father?" she asked, puzzled.

"Did you think you could simply confess and walk away, Laura? That you could violate your marriage vows without consequences?"

Laura's heart pounded. How did he know her name? She'd never given it during the confession, and she didn't think she'd ever spoken with this priest before.

And why was he being so…so cruel?

"I can help you, Laura," he said, his voice suddenly soft. "I can show you a better way."

"I…I don't understand." Her throat was tight, her mouth dry.

"Follow me, and I will show you. There's something better for you—something you can't even imagine."

The gentleness of his tone made her want to believe him, to believe that he genuinely cared and wanted what was best for her. But then she thought of how he'd spoken to her a few moments earlier—the condescension in his voice, the condemnation.

Something about this priest was wrong. He wanted something from her…and she sensed it would be very dangerous to give it to him.

She stood abruptly, her knees shaking. "I'm sorry, I shouldn't have come."

Laura's trembling fingers fumbled with the door handle, twisting it frantically. The wood creaked, but the door remained stubbornly shut. Panic clawed at her throat as she spun around, searching for another way out.

"Going somewhere?" The priest's voice had lost all pretense of warmth. It was cold, hard, like a knife's edge.

"Please," Laura whispered, her back pressed against the confessional wall. "I need to leave."

"Leave?" The priest chuckled, a sound devoid of humor. "You think you can just cast me aside like that, Laura? When I'm showing you a better way?"

Her eyes darted to the latticed window separating them. Through the intricate pattern, she caught a glimpse of movement. The rustle of robes. The glint of something metallic.

"How do you know my name?" she asked, her voice quavering. "I never told you."

Silence stretched between them, broken only by Laura's ragged breathing. Then, slowly, deliberately, the small door in the lattice slid open.

Laura's heart hammered against her ribs as she peered into the darkness of the priest's side. At first, she saw nothing. Then, a face emerged from the shadows, hidden beneath a deep cowl.

"I know many things, Laura," the figure said. "I know about your betrayal. Your lies. Your *weakness*."

She shook her head, tears welling in her eyes. "No, you can't... This isn't right. You're not a real priest, are you?"

Another chuckle, this one sending chills down her spine. "I'm as real as the guilt you carry. As real as the vows you broke."

How could he know? Who was this man?

Her thoughts were interrupted by the sound of a key turning in a lock. The door to the priest's side of the confessional swung open.

She pressed herself further into the corner, her breathing shallow and quick. Fight or flight instincts warred within her as the robed figure stepped into view.

In his hand, he gripped a heavy brass candlestick.

"What are you doing?" Laura asked, her voice barely above a whisper. "Please, just let me go. I won't tell anyone about this."

The priest took a step closer, his face still hidden in shadow. "No, you won't. You're good at keeping secrets, aren't you?"

Laura's eyes darted around the small space, desperately searching for an escape. But there was nowhere to run, nowhere to hide.

"I made a mistake," she said. "I'm sorry. I'll make it right, I promise."

"Promises." The priest spat the word like a curse. "What value do your promises have now, Laura? I gave you a chance to redeem yourself, to choose rightly, but you turned me down. You've left me with no choice."

What was he talking about? What chance had he given her?

He took another step forward, raising the candlestick. Laura could see her terrified reflection in its polished surface.

"No, please," she whimpered, her voice barely audible. "Don't do this."

The priest paused, the candlestick hovering in the air between them. For a moment, hope fluttered in Laura's chest. Maybe he would reconsider. Maybe this nightmare would end.

But then he spoke, his voice low and filled with a terrible purpose. "It's time I showed you the error of your ways, Laura. Time you understood the true weight of your sins."

Laura's eyes widened in horror as the candlestick began its downward arc. Time seemed to slow. She could see every detail: the play of light on the brass, the tensing of the priest's arm, the inevitable path toward her unprotected head.

Something in her snapped. With a surge of adrenaline, she lunged forward, her shoulder connecting with the priest's midsection. The unexpected move caught him off balance, and he stumbled backward, the candlestick clattering to the floor.

Emboldened, Laura scrambled past him, her fingers clawing at the door. It was still locked, so she slammed her body against it repeatedly. The wood creaked and groaned under the assault.

Behind her, the priest groaned, his angry breaths filling the small space. "You can't escape your sins, Laura," he said.

Laura's eyes darted around, searching for a weapon. She spotted the fallen candlestick and dove for it.

The priest lunged at the same moment. Their hands grappled for the brass object, a frantic tug-of-war in the confined space of the confessional.

Laura's fingers closed around the cool metal. With a yell of defiance, she swung it upward, aiming for the priest's cowled head.

But the priest was quicker. He jerked back, narrowly avoiding the blow. In the same motion, his hand shot out, grabbing Laura's wrist and twisting it painfully.

She cried out, the candlestick slipping from her grasp. The priest's other hand clamped over her mouth, muffling her screams.

"Enough," he hissed, his face inches from hers. "It's time to face judgment."

Laura's eyes blazed with fury and fear as she struggled against his grip. She wouldn't give up. She couldn't. But as the priest's hand tightened around her throat, darkness began to creep in at the edges of her vision.

Her last conscious thought was a silent plea for help, for salvation, for one more chance to make things right.

Then the priest's free hand found the candlestick and raised it. It froze overhead for one long, terrible moment.

And then came crashing down.

CHAPTER ONE

"Eddie Mills," Sheila whispered, her heart pounding.

"I wondered when you'd find me," he said, his tired eyes suddenly alert.

For a heartbeat, they stood frozen, eyes locked in the hallway of the nursing home. The bouquet of flowers in Eddie's hand trembled slightly, betraying his nervousness.

In that moment, the weight of Sheila's long quest crashed over her. For years, she'd been haunted by her mother's unsolved murder, a case that had driven her to join the sheriff's department. She'd eventually found footage of the car that had fled the property the night of her mother's murder, and she'd tracked the car to its owner, a criminal named Rayland Bax. But Bax hadn't been in the car that night. According to him, a friend of his had been borrowing the vehicle.

Eddie Mills, a local troublemaker with a history of drug abuse.

After months of dead ends, she'd tracked down Eddie's godmother, Estella Wright, hoping for a lead on his whereabouts.

She'd never expected to literally bump into him here at the nursing home, though.

The chance encounter felt like fate, a moment Sheila had both dreaded and longed for. This man might hold the key to unlocking the mystery that had defined her life and career. The air between them crackled with tension, loaded with unspoken accusations and the promise of long-awaited answers.

"You know who I am?" she asked.

"I do." He swallowed, his throat bobbing. The silence stretched taut, ready to snap.

"Why don't we just head down to the station and talk about—"

Before she could finish, Eddie was in motion, hurling the bouquet of flowers at Sheila's face before bolting down the hallway.

Sheila batted away the flowers, petals scattering across the worn linoleum. "Stop! Police!" she shouted, breaking into a run.

Eddie crashed through a set of double doors, knocking over a cart of medical supplies. Sheila leaped over the scattered debris, her boots skidding as she rounded the corner.

Ahead, a group of elderly patients shuffled along, walkers scraping against the floor. Eddie weaved between them, nearly toppling an old man. Sheila slowed, carefully maneuvering through the group.

"Excuse me, sorry," she muttered, trying not to lose sight of her quarry.

As she broke free of the cluster, a nurse pushing a wheelchair appeared from a side room. Sheila swerved, her shoulder clipping the doorframe. She gritted her teeth against the pain and pushed on.

Eddie glanced back, his eyes wild. He reached a stack of boxes and sent them tumbling. But Sheila didn't slow. She vaulted over the falling cardboard, landing hard but maintaining her momentum.

She wasn't going to let this bastard get away. Not now, not after all the years of waiting and wondering.

Ahead, a door marked "Parking Garage" loomed. Eddie slammed into it, disappearing from view. Sheila burst through seconds later, the cool air of the garage a shock after the stuffy hallways.

She skidded to a stop, scanning the dimly lit space. Concrete pillars cast long shadows, and the acrid smell of exhaust hung in the air.

Eddie was nowhere in sight.

"Damn it," Sheila muttered, straining to hear any sound of movement. Her breath came in ragged gasps, her heart thundering in her ears. She was so close to answers about her mother's death. She couldn't lose him now.

A sudden screech of tires echoed through the garage. Sheila spun toward the sound just as headlights blazed to life, blinding her. A car engine roared, and the vehicle lurched forward, bearing down on her.

Sheila's training kicked in. She dove to the side, feeling the rush of air as the car missed her by inches. She hit the ground hard, rolling to absorb the impact.

In an instant, she was back on her feet, her weapon drawn. But the car was already speeding away, tires squealing as it took a corner. Sheila knew she didn't have a clear shot.

Instead, she focused on the retreating vehicle, burning the license plate into her memory. JRK 4729.

I got you, you bastard, she thought.

***

Sheila slumped into the chair across from Finn's desk, exhaustion finally catching up with her. The adrenaline from her encounter with Eddie had worn off, leaving her drained.

"So, you actually saw him?" Finn asked, leaning forward, his hazel eyes intense.

Sheila nodded, running a hand through her disheveled hair. "Face to face. But he bolted before I could question him. I chased him through the nursing home, but he got away in the parking garage."

"Well, good thing you got the plates," Finn murmured.

Sheila nodded. "I've checked his usual hangouts, talked to his known associates. Nothing. I'm hoping he makes a mistake with the vehicle."

Finn ran a hand through his sandy hair. "We'll find him, Sheila. The whole department's on alert now. It's just a matter of time."

A moment of silence fell between them. Sheila could feel the weight of unspoken words hanging in the air. During their last case, Finn had told her he loved her. The confession had caught her off guard, and they hadn't really addressed it since. The memory of that moment flashed in her mind, bringing with it a mix of confusion and warmth.

They were dating, yes…but exactly how serious was this relationship? How far into the future was Finn looking?

"How's Star doing?" Finn asked, breaking the silence.

Sheila sighed, grateful for the change of subject but also reminded of another responsibility weighing on her. "She's...adjusting. It's not easy for a fourteen-year-old to suddenly have a new home, especially after what she's been through with her father."

"You're doing a good thing, taking her in," Finn said softly, his eyes reflecting admiration and something else Sheila couldn't quite define.

"I hope so," Sheila said, doubt creeping into her voice. "I just wish I knew if I was doing it right. She's just so difficult to get to know, like there's always an invisible wall between us."

Finn leaned back in his chair, suppressing a smile. "Reminds me of someone I know."

Sheila rolled her eyes at him. "I'm serious."

"So am I. And that's why you're probably the best person to help her through everything she's going through."

They both fell silent, pondering this.

Finn cleared his throat, his demeanor growing more official. "There's something else we need to discuss," he said. "The department's starting to look for a permanent replacement for Natalie. Hank doesn't want the job long-term."

Sheila felt a pang in her chest at the mention of her sister's name. Natalie had been the golden child: straight-A student, Olympic gold medalist in kickboxing, and finally, the youngest sheriff Coldwater County had ever seen.

Until the shooting that left her in a wheelchair, and the depression that ultimately led to her taking her own life.

The memory of Natalie's struggle and eventual suicide still haunted Sheila. Sheila had tried to understand what her sister was going through, but Natalie had never confided her struggles in her younger sister, never let Sheila know just how bleak her worldview had grown.

Not until Sheila found her lifeless on the floor of her cabin.

"They're big shoes to fill," Sheila murmured.

"You know, a lot of people think you'd be perfect for the job," Finn said, watching her reaction closely.

Sheila shook her head, a bitter laugh escaping her lips. "I'm not Natalie, Finn. I never have been. She was the achiever, the one everyone looked up to. I'm just...me."

"No, you're not Natalie," Finn agreed. "You're Sheila. And that's more than good enough. Look at how you've handled the Star situation, or how you've pursued your mother's investigation. Natalie would be proud of you."

Their eyes met, and suddenly the air felt charged. As she met her partner's eyes, Sheila thought about Finn's confession to her during their last investigation: 'I love you.' What had he meant by those words? Had he merely spoken in the heat of the moment…or had he been feeling it for a while before he said it?

Finn relented, throwing up his hands and leaning back. "I'm not telling you what to do. If you don't want the job, that's fine. Just thought I'd mention it."

Sheila opened her mouth to respond, but hesitated. The weight of Natalie's legacy, her own ambitions, and her complicated feelings for Finn all swirled in her mind. Before she could formulate a response, the shrill ring of Finn's desk phone cut through the tension.

Finn snatched up the receiver. "Mercer," he answered. His expression shifted from annoyance to concern as he listened. "Slow down, dispatch. What's the situation?"

Sheila leaned forward, her own troubles momentarily forgotten as she watched Finn's face grow increasingly grave.

"We're on our way," Finn said, hanging up the phone. He stood quickly, grabbing his jacket. "We've got a situation at St. Michael's Church."

"What kind of situation?" Sheila asked, already on her feet.

"Possible homicide," Finn replied grimly. "Woman was found beaten to death in the confessional."

CHAPTER TWO

Sheila and Finn raced through Coldwater County, their patrol car slicing through the crisp Utah evening. The sun hung low on the horizon, painting the sky in brilliant hues of orange and pink that reflected off the Great Salt Lake in the distance.

As they sped past familiar landmarks, Sheila couldn't help but feel a disconnect between the beauty of her hometown and the grim reality of their destination.

Coldwater County had always been a place of contrasts. To the north, snow-capped mountains rose majestically, while to the south, the iconic red-rock desert stretched as far as the eye could see. It was a land that attracted both rugged outdoorsmen and tech entrepreneurs, a place where traditional values collided with modern aspirations.

They passed the Coldwater Community College, its modern glass buildings a stark contrast to the old-fashioned main street that formed the heart of their small town. Students milled about, blissfully unaware of the tragedy unfolding just a few miles away.

"I can't believe this is happening here," Sheila murmured, her eyes fixed on the road ahead. "A murder in St. Michael's? It doesn't seem real."

Finn nodded grimly. "I know what you mean. This town's had its share of troubles, but nothing like this."

As they drove, Sheila's mind wandered to the victim. Who was she? What had brought her to the church on this fateful evening? And most chillingly, who had wanted her dead?

They turned onto Church Street, which was lined with quaint houses and well-manicured lawns. Children's bicycles lay abandoned in driveways, testament to the sense of safety that had, until now, defined life in Coldwater County. At the end of the street stood St. Michael's, its weathered stone facade and tall spire a familiar sight to all who called this place home.

As they pulled up to the church, Sheila noticed a small crowd gathering at the police tape that had already been set up. Concerned faces peered at them as they exited the car, whispers rippling through the onlookers. News traveled fast in a small town like theirs.

"Deputy Stone! Deputy Mercer!" a voice called out. It was Mrs. Hendricks, an elderly woman who was a permanent fixture at the popular Steinhart Bar and Grill, her face etched with worry. "Is it true? Has someone really been murdered?"

Sheila approached her, keeping her voice low and calm. "We're still investigating, Mrs. Hendricks. Please, everyone needs to stay back and let us do our job."

As she turned back to Finn, Sheila caught sight of Father Stephen standing near the church entrance, his usually jovial face ashen with shock. He was a prominent member of the community, and though Sheila didn't know him particularly well, she had run into him at a few town meetings.

She and Finn made their way over to the priest, ducking under the police tape.

"Father," Finn said solemnly. "Can you tell us what happened?"

The priest shook his head, as if trying to clear it. "I...I was in my office, preparing for evening mass. I heard a noise from the sanctuary, but I thought nothing of it at first. People often come in to pray." He paused, swallowing hard. "But then I heard a scream. By the time I got there...it was too late."

Sheila placed a comforting hand on the priest's shoulder. "You did everything you could, Father. Can you show us where you found her?"

Father Stephen nodded, leading them into the church. The heavy wooden doors creaked as they entered, the sound echoing ominously through the silent sanctuary. The familiar scent of incense hung in the air, now tainted with something metallic and unsettling.

As they approached the confessional, Sheila's trained eye took in every detail. Nothing seemed out of place in the main area of the church. The pews stood in neat rows, hymnals and Bibles tucked tidily in their places. Candles flickered softly at the altar, casting long shadows across the stone floor.

The confessional, too, looked normal, the latticed window holding nothing but darkness within. The only sign that anything might be wrong was the faint line of blood visible just beneath the door.

"The body's still inside," said a voice behind them. Sheila turned to see Dr. Jin Zihao, the county coroner, approaching. His usually immaculate appearance was disheveled, a testament to the urgency of the situation.

"What can you tell us, Doc?" Finn asked.

Dr. Zihao's sharp eyes met theirs. "Female victim, late thirties to early forties. The cause of death appears to be blunt force trauma to the head and upper body. I'll know more after the autopsy, but from the initial examination, I'd say she was beaten to death."

Sheila felt a chill run down her spine. "Beaten to death in a confessional," she murmured. "What kind of monster would do something like this?"

They stepped closer to the confessional, and Sheila steeled herself for what she was about to see. The victim's body lay crumpled in the small space, her features barely recognizable beneath the bruising and blood.

For just a moment, Sheila felt herself transported back to her sister's cabin. She closed her eyes and clenched her fists, willing the moment to pass, willing herself to remain rooted here in this church.

And then the feeling was gone.

Taking a relieved breath, she scanned the confessional. She spotted something partially hidden beneath the victim's body—a heavy brass candlestick. Its ornate surface was smeared with blood and what looked like strands of hair.

"Finn," she called softly. "I think we've found our murder weapon."

Finn leaned in for a closer look. "Looks that way. We'll have forensics bag it for evidence."

As they stepped back to allow the crime scene technicians to do their work, Sheila turned her attention back to the priest. "Father Stephen," she said, "have you seen this woman before?"

The priest swallowed hard, looking away from the confessional. "I can't be certain, not with...with the state she's in," he said, his voice shaking. "But I believe it's Laura Hastings. She's a parishioner here, comes to confession regularly. Well, she used to—I haven't seen her in a number of months."

Sheila jotted down the name in her notebook. "Thank you, Father. That's very helpful."

"Are there any cameras in or around the church, by any chance?" Finn asked, looking around.

Father Stephen smiled sadly. "I'm afraid we're not quite that modern. I don't believe there are any cameras on neighboring properties, either."

"Did Laura have any enemies that you know of?" Sheila asked. "Anyone who might want to harm her?"

Father Stephen shook his head. "No, not that I know of. Laura was...troubled, certainly. She carried a great burden of guilt. But she was a kind soul. I can't imagine anyone wanting to hurt her."

Sheila's brow furrowed. "Guilt? What do you mean by that, Father?"

The priest hesitated, his eyes darting between Sheila and Finn. "I...I'm not sure I should say. What's shared in confession is meant to be confidential."

"Father, I understand your position," Finn said, "but Laura is dead now. You might know something that could help us find her killer and bring them to justice."

Father Stephen sighed heavily, his shoulders sagging under the weight of his decision. After a long moment, he spoke. "Laura was having...marital problems. She mentioned thinking about leaving her husband."

Sheila jotted this down in her notebook. "Did she say why she was considering leaving him?"

The priest shook his head. "No, she never went into specifics. Just that she was unhappy and felt trapped. But she was torn about it—hence the guilt. She believed strongly in the sanctity of marriage."

Sheila nodded, processing this information. Then a thought struck her. "Father, was her confession scheduled?"

"Not as far as I know," Father Stephen said, looking puzzled. "Which is odd, since they're supposed to be scheduled."

"Were any other priests taking confession today?" Finn asked.

The priest shook his head again. "No, I'm the only priest here."

Sheila and Finn exchanged a look.

"Thank you, Father Stephen," Sheila said. "Let us know if you think of anything else."

The priest nodded and turned away. When he was out of earshot, Sheila said, "So why was Laura here? Did she meet with someone else?"

"You know what they say," Finn said. "When in doubt, question the spouse."

She raised a skeptical eyebrow. "Is that really a saying?"

He shrugged. "No. But it should be. Maybe he found out she was thinking of leaving, flipped out."

"But if so, why attack her here, in a public place?"

"Guess we'd better ask him that."

CHAPTER THREE

The Hastings residence was a modest two-story home on Maple Street, its well-manicured lawn and cheerful flower beds at odds with the tragedy that had befallen its occupants. As Sheila and Finn approached the front door, the weight of their task hung heavy in the air.

Sheila took a deep breath before ringing the doorbell. The sound echoed through the house, followed by the muffled sound of footsteps. After a moment, the door opened to reveal a man in his early forties, his eyes red-rimmed and his clothes rumpled.

"Mr. Hastings?" Sheila asked gently. At his nod, she continued, "I'm Deputy Sheila Stone, and this is my partner, Deputy Finn Mercer. We're here about your wife, Laura. May we come in?"

James Hastings stepped back, gesturing for them to enter. His movements were slow, almost mechanical, as if he were moving through a thick fog. "Of course," he murmured. "Please, have a seat."

The living room was cozy and neat, with family photos lining the walls. One of the photos depicted Laura at a community event at the library—a fundraiser, by the look of it—where she was surrounded by a crowd of smiling faces, but the photograph that really caught Sheila's attention was a large portrait above the fireplace: Laura Hastings, smiling brightly, her arms wrapped around her husband. The contrast between the vibrant woman in the photo and the broken man before them was striking.

As they sat on the sofa, James collapsed into an armchair across from them. "I still can't believe it," he said. "Laura...she can't be gone. It doesn't feel real."

Sheila leaned forward. "Mr. Hastings, we're very sorry for your loss. We know this is difficult, but we need to ask you some questions, if that's okay with you."

James nodded, running a hand through his disheveled hair. "Of course. Anything to help find who...who did this to Laura."

Finn pulled out his notebook. "Can you tell us about your relationship with Laura? How long were you married?"

"Fifteen years," James replied, a ghost of a smile flickering across his face. "We met in college. It was...it was love at first sight, you know? At least for me." His smile faded, replaced by a look of deep sorrow. "Lately, though, things have been...strained."

Sheila pursed her lips, curious. "Strained how, Mr. Hastings?"

James sighed heavily. "Laura had been distant. Secretive. I thought maybe...maybe she was seeing someone else. I confronted her about it last week, but she denied it. Said she just needed some space to figure things out."

Sheila exchanged a glance with Finn. This aligned with what Father Stephen had told them about Laura considering leaving her husband. "Did Laura mention anything about wanting to leave you, Mr. Hastings?"

James looked up sharply, pain etched across his features. "Leave me? No, she never...I mean, I knew things weren't great, but I didn't think..." He trailed off, his eyes filling with tears. "Oh God, was she really going to leave me?"

Sheila's heart went out to the man, but she had to press on. "Mr. Hastings, where were you earlier this evening? Around, say, five o'clock?"

"I was at work," James replied, wiping his eyes. "I'm an accountant at Elbridge College. We're in the middle of budget season, so I've been working late. You can check with my colleagues. I didn't leave the office until after ten."

Finn made a note of this. "We'll need to verify that, of course."

James nodded. "Of course. I understand."

As Sheila watched James, she couldn't shake the feeling that his grief was genuine. While she knew appearances could be deceiving, her instincts told her that this man wasn't their killer.

"Mr. Hastings," she said gently, "did you know Laura was going to confession earlier this evening?"

James nodded. "Yes, she mentioned she was going to the church, and I admit I was a bit surprised. We're not...we weren't very religious."

Sheila leaned forward. "Did she say anything about why she was going?"

James hesitated, furrowing his brow. "I...I'm not sure. Laura's been so closed off lately. She didn't share much with me."

"Try to remember, Mr. Hastings," Finn said. "Even the smallest detail could be important."

James shook his head, frustration evident in his voice. "I'm sorry, I just can't... It's all a blur. The last few weeks, the arguments, and now this... I can barely think straight."

Sheila exchanged a glance with Finn. They needed more information, but pushing too hard might shut James down completely. She decided to try a different approach.

"Mr. Hastings," she said softly, "I know this is incredibly difficult. But think back to the last time you and Laura talked about her going to church. Was there anything unusual? Anything that stood out?"

James closed his eyes, his hands clenching and unclenching in his lap. For a long moment, he was silent, and Sheila worried they'd hit a dead end. Then, suddenly, his eyes snapped open.

"Wait," he said, his voice barely above a whisper. "There was something. Laura mentioned…she needed to talk to someone. Someone she could trust."

"At the church?" Finn asked.

James nodded slowly. "Yes, at the church. She seemed...relieved. Like she'd found someone who could help her."

Sheila leaned in, her heart racing. They were close to something, she could feel it. "Did she mention who this person was, Mr. Hastings?"

James's face scrunched up in concentration. "I think...I think it was a priest. But not the usual one. Someone new."

"Do you remember a name?" Finn asked, his pen poised over his notebook.

James shook his head, then stopped. "Wait. It was something...something like...Wayland? Yes, Father Wayland, I think. Laura seemed to trust him."

Sheila felt a surge of triumph, quickly tempered by the gravity of the situation. "You're sure about that name? Father Wayland?"

"Pretty sure," James replied, looking somewhat more confident. "Why? Is that important?"

"We're not sure yet," Sheila said, careful not to reveal too much. She doubted James had been given many details about his wife's murder, and she didn't want to plant any seeds of suspicion in his mind.

"What else can you tell us about this, Father Wayland?" she asked.

James shrugged helplessly. "Nothing, really. Laura didn't say much about him, just that he was new and that she felt comfortable talking to him. I...I was just glad she had someone to talk to, you know? Even if it wasn't me."

Sheila glanced at Finn. They needed to talk to Father Stephen again, see if he knew anything about this Father Wayland. Could the killer be a local priest, or had he merely been posing as a priest?

As they stood to leave, Sheila placed a comforting hand on James's shoulder. "We'll find who did this, Mr. Hastings. I promise you that."

James nodded, his eyes hollow with grief. "Thank you. Just...please, find out why. Why Laura? She was the kindest person I knew. Who could do something like this?"

Outside, as they walked to their car, Finn turned to Sheila. "What do you think?"

Sheila sighed, running a hand through her hair. "I think James Hastings is genuinely devastated by his wife's death. And if he really was at work until after ten, there's no way he could have killed Laura."

Finn nodded in agreement. "So that leaves this Father Wayland. Maybe Father Stephen can tell us who he is."

As they reached their car, Sheila's phone rang. She glanced at the screen, not recognizing the number. "Deputy Stone," she answered.

"Deputy, my name is Jonah Tournay," a male voice said, sounding tense and uncomfortable. "I need your help."

Sheila put the phone on speaker so Finn could hear. "What about, Mr. Tournay?"

"My sister, Sophie," Jonah replied, his voice cracking. "She's been missing for three days...and the last thing I knew, she was meeting with a priest."

"I'm so sorry, Mr. Tournay," Sheila said, her voice filled with concern. "Can you tell us more about your sister's disappearance?"

Jonah's voice trembled as he spoke. "I...I heard about the murder at St. Michael's on the news, and it got me thinking about Sophie. She told me she was meeting with a priest, and then…then she vanished."

Finn and Sheila exchanged a worried glance. The connection was too strong to ignore.

"Mr. Tournay," Finn said, "this is Deputy Mercer. We'd like to speak with you in person. Would that be possible?"

There was a brief pause before Jonah replied, "Yes, of course. Anything to help find Sophie."

"Great," Sheila said, trying to keep her voice calm and reassuring. "How about we meet at Steinhart's in half an hour?"

"I'll be there," Jonah said, and the call ended.

Sheila glanced at Finn, who was already watching her. "What are you thinking?" he asked.

"I'm thinking we may have a serial killer on our hands," she said. "And I'm also thinking that if we're not careful, Sophie Tournay might end up like Laura Hastings—if she hasn't already."

CHAPTER FOUR

Steinhart's Bar and Grill was a cozy local spot, its large windows offering a view of Coldwater's main street. As Sheila and Finn entered, the familiar scent of grilled meats enveloped them. The restaurant was bustling with the evening crowd, locals catching up over burgers and craft beers.

They spotted Jonah immediately, a man in his early thirties with worried eyes and disheveled brown hair. He sat alone at a corner table, nervously fidgeting with a paper napkin.

Sheila studied Jonah Tournay across the table, taking in his nervous demeanor and the dark circles under his eyes. Finn sat beside her, his notebook open and ready.

"Mr. Tournay," Sheila began, "thank you for meeting with us. We understand how difficult this must be."

Jonah nodded, his hands wrapped tightly around a steaming mug of coffee. "I just want to find my sister," he said, his voice barely above a whisper.

Sheila glanced around and noticed Mrs. Hendricks at a nearby table, pretending to read a newspaper while obviously eavesdropping. In a small town like Coldwater, news traveled fast, and Mrs. Hendricks was known as the local gossip hub.

That's the last thing we need, Sheila thought. *Someone figuring out that Sophie's disappearance might be related to Laura's death—and terrifying the whole town.*

Sheila caught Finn's eye and gave a subtle nod toward Mrs. Hendricks. Finn understood immediately. He stood up, smoothing his uniform.

"Mr. Tournay, if you'll excuse me for a moment," Finn said politely before making his way to Mrs. Hendricks' table.

"Mrs. Hendricks," he said warmly, "I'm so glad I ran into you. I was hoping to speak with you about the neighborhood watch program. Do you have a moment?"

Mrs. Hendricks blinked, puzzled. "The neighborhood watch program? What could that possibly have to do with me?"

"A lot, in fact. Why don't we go over to a table by the wall where it's quieter? I'd love to pick your brain about…"

That was all Sheila caught. Then Finn was leading a bewildered Mrs. Hendricks across the room, where there was no risk of her eavesdropping on Sheila's conversation with Jonah.

Sheila cleared her throat and turned her attention back to Jonah.

"I apologize for the interruption, Mr. Tournay," she said. "What can you tell me about Sophie? What's she like?"

Jonah's eyes softened, a small smile tugging at his lips despite the worry etched on his face. "Sophie's...she's amazing. Kind, smart, always helping others. She volunteers at the local shelter, teaches Sunday school. She's very religious, has been since we were kids."

"How old is she?" Sheila asked, jotting down notes.

"She just turned twenty-nine last month," Jonah replied. "We had a small party for her at our parents' house. She seemed happy then, but looking back...I think something was bothering her."

Sheila leaned forward, curious. "What makes you say that?"

Jonah sighed, running a hand through his hair. "It's hard to explain. Sophie's always been...I don't know, serene? But that day, she seemed distracted. Like she was carrying a weight on her shoulders."

"And you said she was meeting with a priest?" Sheila asked, keeping her voice low to avoid attracting attention.

Jonah nodded. "Yeah, she mentioned it last week. Said she needed to talk to someone about...about something she'd done."

Sheila kept her expression neutral, but her mind was racing with the parallels to Laura Hastings' case. "What do you mean, Mr. Tournay?"

Jonah shifted uncomfortably in his seat, his eyes darting around the restaurant before leaning in closer. "Sophie...she made a mistake. A big one. She was really torn up about it."

"What kind of mistake?"

Jonah sighed heavily, his shoulders slumping. "She...she had an affair. With a married man. It was brief, but Sophie was devastated. Said she'd betrayed everything she believed in."

The revelation hung in the air between them. Sheila felt a chill run down her spine as she remembered Laura Hastings' marital troubles. Was it possible the killer's MO involved infidelity? But if so, why not target the married man Sophie had cheated with?

You're getting ahead of yourself. As far as you know, Sophie's disappearance may have nothing to do with Laura's death.

"Did Sophie tell you who the man was?" Sheila asked, keeping her voice low.

Jonah shook his head. "No, she wouldn't say. She *did* tell me she was torn up about it, though."

Sheila nodded. "And that's when she mentioned meeting with the priest?"

"Yeah," Jonah said. "She said she needed guidance, needed to make things right with God. She said she was too embarrassed to talk with her own priest—he knows the person she had an affair with. She wanted to speak with someone outside the situation...and I guess this priest fit the bill."

"Did Sophie tell you where she was meeting this priest?" Sheila asked, hoping for a solid lead.

Jonah furrowed his brow in concentration. "Chester's, I think? It's a bar at the west end of town."

"I know it. Seems like an odd place to meet a priest."

"That's what I thought, too. She said he wasn't like most priests—not as strict."

Sheila made a note of that. "Did she mention the priest's name, by any chance?"

Jonah shook his head. "No, just that he was new in town. Someone she felt she could trust."

Another parallel to Laura Hastings' case. Sheila felt the pieces starting to come together, forming a picture she didn't like one bit.

"I must say I'm a bit puzzled," she said. "It's been three days since your sister went missing. How come you didn't say anything about this meeting sooner?"

Jonah sighed. "I've been racking my brain, trying to think of everything Laura said, everything we talked about. I forgot about Chester's until just recently—it seemed like such an insignificant detail at the time. I mean, I love my sister like hell, but I wasn't thinking something terrible might happen to her."

Sheila nodded, absorbing this. "One last question," she said. "When exactly was the last time you saw or heard from Sophie?"

Jonah's face crumpled, the pain of his sister's disappearance evident in every line. "Three days ago. We had lunch together. She seemed...I don't know, both relieved and anxious? She said she was meeting the priest that evening, and that afterward, everything would be okay." His voice broke on the last word. "But she never came home. I've been calling and texting, but there's no response. It's not like her, not at all."

Sheila reached out, placing a comforting hand on Jonah's arm. "We're going to do everything we can to find Sophie, Mr. Tournay. I promise you that."

He nodded, hanging his head as if he already knew something terrible had happened to his sister. Sheila caught Finn's eye as she rose from her seat. Finn broke away from his conversation, and they joined each other at the door, which Finn held open for Sheila.

"Thanks for running interference," Sheila said as they stepped into the cool night air.

"You bet. What'd you find out?"

"Apparently Sophie was supposed to meet an unnamed priest at Chester's Bar and Grill three nights ago. She met her brother for lunch that day, and it was the last time he saw her."

They made their way toward Sheila's vehicle, a standard-issue Ford Explorer painted in the department's distinctive black and gold colors. The vehicle was equipped with all the necessary law enforcement gear, including a reinforced push bumper, emergency lights, and a siren. Despite its official appearance, however, Sheila had made the interior her own over the years. A small photo of her sister Natalie was tucked into the sun visor, and a well-worn kickboxing glove hung from the rearview mirror, subtle reminders of her past and her motivation to serve and protect.

"There's something else," Sheila added as she climbed into the driver's seat. "Sophie Tournay had an affair with a married man."

Finn slid into the passenger seat. "You think that's the connection?"

"Could be. Both victims were religious, two."

"Sounds like we know our killer's MO: He targets religious women who've committed some kind of...marital sin, I guess."

"Maybe the killer sees himself as some kind of moral enforcer," she said, pulling out onto the street.

"A vigilante priest," Finn mused, his tone skeptical. "Considering the state of marriages these days, he's not going to run out of targets any time soon."

"All the more reason to stop him as soon as possible. Come on, let's head over to Chester's. Maybe we'll find someone who remembers seeing him."

CHAPTER FIVE

Sheila's fingers drummed an anxious rhythm on the steering wheel as she guided the SUV through Coldwater's deserted streets. The clock on the dashboard read 12:37 AM, but sleep was the furthest thing from her mind. Every second that ticked by was another moment Sophie Tournay might be in danger.

If she was still alive at all.

"You okay?" Finn asked from the passenger seat, his voice cutting through the tense silence.

Sheila glanced at him, forcing a tight smile. "Just thinking about Sophie. And Laura. And how this whole mess feels like it's spinning out of control. I mean, if the man Sophie was meeting with is the same person who killed Laura, that's a gap of only three nights. Will he attack someone else in three nights?"

"You're assuming he attacked Sophie at all. For all we know, she could be safe and sound."

Sheila studied him for a few long seconds before turning her attention back to the road. "You don't really think that," she said.

Finn sighed. "It never hurts to be optimistic, does it?"

Sheila slowed the SUV as they neared Chester's Bar and Grill. The neon sign cast a dim, reddish glow over the nearly empty parking lot, the flickering 'R' giving the place an eerie, abandoned feel.

"Not exactly bustling," Finn said as they stepped out of the SUV.

Sheila shrugged, her eyes scanning the area. "We just need to find one person who was here three nights ago, that's it."

They entered the bar, the smell of stale beer and fried food hitting them immediately. A few patrons lingered at the bar, nursing their drinks in silence. Country music played softly from an old jukebox in the corner, the melancholy tune fitting the mood perfectly.

The bartender, a middle-aged man with a receding hairline and a faded tattoo on his forearm, looked up as they approached. "We're about to close up," he said, his tone weary.

Sheila flashed her badge. "Deputy Stone, Coldwater County Sheriff's Department. This is Deputy Mercer. We need to ask a few questions about a patron who was here three nights ago."

The bartender sighed, setting down the glass he'd been cleaning. "Three nights ago? Sorry, but I wasn't working then."

"Is there anyone here who *was* working then?" Sheila asked.

The bartender thought for a moment, his brow furrowed. "Well, Irene was on shift. She's in the kitchen now, closing up."

Sheila and Finn exchanged a look of renewed hope. "Can we speak with her?" Finn asked.

The bartender shrugged. "Sure, go on back. Just don't get in the way of closing procedures. Boss hates it when we're late locking up."

As they made their way to the kitchen, Sheila couldn't help but notice the worn-down appearance of the place. Faded posters of long-past events clung to the walls, and the floor was sticky beneath her boots. It was the kind of place where secrets could easily be buried, forgotten in the haze of alcohol and dim lighting.

They pushed through the swinging doors into the kitchen. The clanging of pots and the hiss of a cleaning spray filled the air. A petite woman with curly red hair was wiping down a stainless steel counter, her movements quick and efficient.

"Irene?" Sheila asked.

The woman's head snapped up, her eyes widening at the sight of the deputies. "Y-yes?" she stammered, taking a step back. Her hand clutched the cleaning rag tightly, knuckles white with tension.

Sheila held up her hands in a calming gesture. "We're not here to cause trouble. We just need to ask you a few questions about a patron from three nights ago."

Irene's eyes darted between them and the exit. "I don't...I don't know anything. I just serve drinks and food, that's all."

Seems awfully edgy, Sheila thought. *Maybe she's had run-ins with the law before.*

Finn stepped forward, his voice gentle. "This is very important," Finn said. "A woman's life may depend on it."

Irene swallowed hard. "What exactly do you want to know?"

Sheila showed her the photo of Sophie. "Do you remember seeing this woman here?"

Irene studied the photo, recognition dawning in her eyes. "Yeah, I remember her. She was sitting at a corner table, looked kind of nervous. Kept checking her phone."

"Was she meeting someone?" Finn asked.

Irene nodded. "A man. I didn't get a good look at him, though. He was wearing a hat, kept his head down most of the time."

"Can you describe him at all?" Sheila asked, hope rising in her chest.

Irene furrowed her brow. "Um, average height, I guess? Dark clothes. Kind of looked like a politician, you know? Fancy suit and all that."

Sheila nodded, filing this information away. "Do you remember anything else? When did they leave?"

"It was late," Irene said. "We were about to close up. They left together through the side door. The man...he had his hand on her back. It looked...I don't know, possessive?"

Sheila and Finn exchanged a significant look. "Thank you, Irene," Sheila said. "You've been very helpful."

Irene nodded, her face pale. "Is she okay? The woman in the photo?"

Sheila paused, choosing her words carefully. "We're doing everything we can to find her. We appreciate your cooperation."

With that, Sheila and Finn hurried away, returning to the main room of the bar before taking the side door Irene had mentioned. They emerged in a narrow alley. Sheila's eyes scanned the area, looking for anything out of place. The alley was dark, lit only by a single flickering streetlight at the far end. Dumpsters lined one wall, their pungent odor mixing with the lingering smell of fried food from the kitchen.

"Sheila," Finn said suddenly, pointing upward.

Sheila followed his gaze and felt a surge of excitement. There, mounted on the corner of the building, was a security camera.

***

Sheila and Finn made their way back into the bar, where they found a stocky man with a neatly trimmed beard locking the cash register. The jukebox had fallen silent, and the last few patrons were shuffling out the door, leaving behind a silence broken only by the soft clink of glasses being cleaned.

"Excuse me," Sheila said, approaching the stocky man. "Are you the manager?"

The man looked up, his eyes narrowing. "Yeah, that's me. Tom Grayson. What can I do for you?" His tone suggested he'd much rather be left alone.

"I'm Deputy Stone, and this is Deputy Mercer. We're trying to track down someone who was here three nights ago. Can you access the footage from the security camera above the back door?"

Tom shook his head, his expression a mix of annoyance and wariness. "Sorry, but we're closing up. Come back tomorrow during business hours."

"This is an urgent matter, Mr. Grayson," Finn said. "It's very important we find this woman."

Tom's expression hardened. "Look, I sympathize, but I can't just hand over our security footage to anyone who asks. There are protocols, privacy concerns. Unless you have a warrant—"

"We don't have time for a warrant," Sheila said, frustration edging into her voice. "The woman we're looking for could be in danger."

Tom lowered his voice to a more confidential tone. "Is this about what happened at St. Michael's? The whole town's shaken up about that. If there's a killer on the loose..."

Sheila exchanged a glance with Finn. They needed Tom's cooperation, but how much should they reveal? The delicate balance between informing the public and protecting the integrity of the investigation weighed heavily on her mind.

"It's possible there's a connection," she said carefully. "We can't say for certain yet."

"You think this woman you're looking for is dead, too?"

Sheila took a deep breath, acutely aware of the ticking clock in her mind. "We can't disclose all the details of an ongoing investigation, but I can tell you that we're trying to prevent another tragedy. The footage from your camera could be the key to stopping a dangerous individual."

Tom studied them for a long moment, his gaze moving from Sheila to Finn and back again. The silence stretched, broken only by the distant hum of the refrigerators behind the bar. Finally, he sighed, his shoulders sagging slightly. "Alright. Follow me."

He led them through a door marked 'Employees Only' and down a narrow hallway lined with faded posters of long-past events. The smell of stale beer and cleaning products grew stronger as they approached a small office at the end of the corridor.

Inside, a computer was set up with multiple monitors, the screens casting a blue glow over the cluttered desk. Tom sat down in a worn office chair and began typing, navigating through folders to pull up the security footage from three nights earlier.

Sheila and Finn leaned in, their eyes fixed on the screens. The grainy black-and-white footage showed the side entrance of the bar, the timestamp in the corner reading 9:42 PM.

"There," Sheila said, pointing to the screen as two figures appeared in the frame. "That's Sophie."

They watched intently as Sophie left the bar with a man. Just as Irene had described, the man had one hand on Sophie's back, guiding her. But what caught Sheila's attention was his other hand.

"Look," she said to Finn, her voice tight with tension. "He's covering his face."

Sure enough, the man's free hand was held up to his face, as if rubbing his forehead—and effectively obscuring the camera's view.

"He knew about the camera," Finn muttered, his brow furrowing. "Must have scoped out the place beforehand."

Sheila nodded grimly. "This wasn't a spontaneous act. He planned this."

"You telling me some psycho's been casing my place of business?" Tom asked.

"I'm telling you that you should probably keep a close eye on things in case he finds reason to come back," Finn said. "Keep the footage rolling."

They continued watching as Sophie and the man headed not toward the parking lot but toward an adjoining alley.

"That alley," Sheila said, her pulse quickening. "Where does it lead?"

Tom shrugged, looking uncomfortable. "Nowhere, really. It's a dead end. Sometimes people use it to smoke or...you know, get some privacy."

Sheila and Finn exchanged a look, an unspoken understanding passing between them. Without another word, they hurried out of the office, back through the bar, and out the side door, emerging once again into the cool night air.

They crossed to the alley, which was dark, the flickering streetlight barely penetrating the gloom. Sheila pulled out her flashlight, its beam cutting through the shadows like a knife. They moved cautiously, alert for any sound or movement.

The air felt heavy, thick with the scent of rotting garbage from nearby dumpsters and something else...something metallic and sickly sweet that made Sheila's stomach churn with dread.

As they neared the end of the alley, Sheila's light fell on something sprawled on the ground. Her heart leaped into her throat, and she felt Finn tense beside her.

"Finn," she said, her voice barely above a whisper. "Look."

There, half-hidden behind a dumpster, lay a body. The beam of Sheila's flashlight revealed a woman's form, her limbs splayed at unnatural angles. Dark stains spread across her clothing, glistening wetly in the harsh light.

Sheila approached slowly, her training warring with the horror rising in her chest. As she drew closer, she could make out more details: the woman's pale face, her eyes staring sightlessly at the sky, her mouth frozen in a silent scream.

It was, without a doubt, Sophie Tournay.

CHAPTER SIX

The Father sat motionless in his sedan, eyes fixed on the alleyway behind Chester's Bar and Grill.

I wonder what she looks like now, he thought. *Is she as beautiful in death as she was in life?*

The night enveloped him like a shroud, the darkness a comforting presence. He had been sitting here a while, watching as the two police officers entered the bar and then emerged into the alley. He'd heard the report go out over the police radio, and he'd felt…what was that feeling? Satisfaction? Validation?

No—purpose. Meaning.

He knew he ought to drive away, get himself as far from the dead woman's body as possible, but something compelled him to stay. He liked to linger, watching the aftermath unfold, seeing the shock and horror on the faces of those who discovered his handiwork. Watching the news wasn't even close to being there in person.

Besides, it wasn't as if anyone would recognize him. If anyone remembered anything about him, which he found unlikely, it wouldn't matter because he would soon change his appearance.

As he sat there, drinking in the scene, the Father began to remove his disguise. The wig came off first, revealing close-cropped gray hair underneath. He peeled off the prosthetic nose and cheeks that had altered his facial structure. Lastly, he removed the colored contacts, blinking as his natural eye color was restored.

He placed each piece of the disguise in a specialized bag designed to preserve evidence. He would dispose of it all later, in a place far from here. He had been meticulous, leaving no trace of himself behind: no DNA, no fingerprints, nothing that could lead back to him.

Confidence surged through him. They would never catch him. How could they? He was merely an instrument of a higher power, carrying out God's will. Divine protection surrounded him like an impenetrable shield.

The Father closed his eyes, bowing his head slightly. "Lord," he whispered, "I thank you for guiding my hand tonight. May this act of cleansing bring us one step closer to Paradise on Earth. Bless this mission you have entrusted to me, and grant me the strength to continue your holy work."

As he finished his prayer, a sense of peace settled over him. He was doing what was right, what was necessary. The world was full of sin, and he was the cleansing fire sent to purify it.

With one last glance at the chaotic scene behind Chester's, the Father started his car. As he pulled away from the curb, blending seamlessly into the sparse late-night traffic, his mind was already turning to his next target.

After all, his work was far from over. There were so many more sinners to judge, so many more souls to send to their final reckoning.

And he, the Father, would be there to deliver God's justice, one sinner at a time.

CHAPTER SEVEN

Finn watched as Sheila stepped away from Sophie's body, her face a mask of shock and grief. He'd seen that look before in the days following Natalie's suicide, and it worried him deeply.

She hasn't gotten over it, he thought. *Then again, it's been less than a year...and besides, do you* ever *get over something like your sister's suicide?*

He felt an urge to follow her, to try to help her work through whatever she was dealing with, but he couldn't just leave the body unattended. First and foremost, he needed to secure the crime scene.

As he dialed dispatch to call in the discovery, Finn found himself reflecting on how different Sheila had been since her sister's death. The vibrant, determined woman he'd grown to admire seemed to be slipping away, replaced by someone haunted and withdrawn.

Would she always be like this? And if so...what did that mean for their future? At the risk of sounding cruel, could he really build a life with someone who seemed so stuck in the past?

The call went through, and he cleared his throat. "Dispatch, this is Deputy Mercer. We've got a 187 in the alley behind Chester's Bar and Grill. Victim is Sophie Tournay. We need forensics and the M.E. here ASAP."

As he spoke, Finn began securing the crime scene, his movements automatic after years on the job. He unrolled the yellow crime scene tape, cordoning off the area with practiced efficiency. His mind, however, was elsewhere, grappling with his feelings for Sheila and his fears for their future.

He glanced over at her. She was now leaning against the alley wall, her eyes closed, taking deep breaths. The sight of her, so visibly shaken, tugged at Finn's heart, and he found himself making his way over to her.

"Sheila," he said softly, reaching out to touch her arm. "Are you okay?"

Her eyes snapped open, a mix of emotions swirling in their depths. "I'm fine," she said, straightening her shoulders.

Finn didn't buy it. "It's okay not to be fine, you know. This is a tough case, and finding Sophie like this..."

She swallowed hard, as if unsure what to say. "Let's just...just focus on the job, okay? Please?"

Finn held up his hands in surrender, recognizing there was nothing more to be done. "Okay," he said. "But I'm here if you need me."

Sheila nodded, then pushed past him and made her way to the mouth of the alley, presumably to flag down the emergency vehicles that would be here soon. Finn watched her go, worry gnawing at his gut. He wanted to help her, to be there for her, but it was clear she wasn't ready to let him in. With a sigh, he turned back to the crime scene, hoping that somehow, solving this case might help Sheila find her way back to herself.

The sound of approaching sirens cut through the night air, growing louder with each passing second. Soon, the alley would be swarming with officers and crime scene technicians. Finn steeled himself for the long night ahead.

His eyes were drawn back to Sophie's body. Now that his eyes had adjusted to the darkness of the alley, he could see her more clearly. Her blonde hair was matted with blood, splayed out around her head like a macabre halo. Her blue eyes, once vibrant with life, now stared blankly at the night sky. Her lips, slightly parted, seemed frozen in a final, silent plea for help.

Finn felt a lump forming in his throat. She looked so young, so vulnerable. He thought of the bright, religious woman Jonah had described, so unlike the broken form before him.

A wave of anger washed over him, followed quickly by a deep sadness. This woman had had her whole life ahead of her, and now she lay discarded in a dirty alley like she was nothing. Finn clenched his fists, a mix of grief and determination surging through him. He silently vowed to find the person responsible for this, to bring some measure of justice to Sophie and her family.

"It never gets easier, does it?"

Finn turned to see Dr. Zihao standing behind him. He hadn't heard the coroner approach, too lost in his examination of Sophie's body. Finn straightened, trying to compose himself.

"No," he agreed, his voice rough with emotion. "It doesn't."

Dr. Zihao nodded solemnly, his experienced eyes already assessing the scene. "Let's see what she can tell us about her final moments," he said quietly, kneeling beside Sophie's body.

Finn stepped back, allowing the coroner to work.

"Cause of death appears to be blunt force trauma to the head," Dr. Zihao said after a few moments. "Likely from a heavy object. There are multiple impact sites, suggesting repeated blows. I'll know more after the autopsy, but the injuries are consistent with those found on Laura Hastings."

Finn nodded, his suspicions confirmed. He felt a chill run down his spine at the thought of the brutality Sophie must have endured in her final moments.

"Think it could've been a candlestick?" Finn asked. They had recovered the candlestick used to kill Laura, of course, but perhaps the killer had more. It might be part of his signature.

"Could be a brick, for all I know," the coroner answered. "I'll have to get her to the lab and examine her properly."

Sheila was hovering a few paces away, looking on with a detached expression, her arms crossed. Finn joined her, and together they retreated a short distance from the body.

"Both killed the same way," Sheila murmured, her voice hollow. "Both religious women, both of them attacked by priests or people pretending to be priests."

It occurred to Finn that, technically speaking, they didn't know that Laura had been attacked by a priest. But, given the fact that she was killed in a confessional and there was no record of who she was supposed to meet with, it seemed the most likely explanation.

Finn nodded. "Both killed in very violent ways, as well. Think it's some kind of punishment?"

"Could be," Sheila murmured, staring thoughtfully at the ground. "Could be taking revenge, too. It's not a very intimate form of killing, though. Not like strangling."

"Maybe it's less personal, then. Maybe it wasn't about these two women in particular—maybe they represent something to the killer."

"Either way, I'd say it's pretty clear we're dealing with the same murderer."

They both fell silent, considering the possibilities.

Just then, something caught Finn's eye. There, half-hidden in the shadows of the alley, was a small, glinting object. He moved closer, crouching down to examine it.

"What is it?" Sheila asked.

"A cuff link." He frowned, holding it up to the glow of the nearby street light. "It has initials on it, too. TB. Who do you think that is?"

"The person who killed Sophie Tournay, more than likely."

***

Back at the station, the buzz of fluorescent lights and the hum of computers filled the air as Sheila and Finn hunched over their desks, deep into their investigation of the mysterious cuff link. The small, silver object sat in an evidence bag between them, its engraved initials "TB" seeming to mock their efforts.

There's gotta be a way to track these down, Finn thought. *But how?*

"Bingo," Sheila said, slapping her phone down on the table. She'd been talking on the phone for the past ten minutes or so, but Finn had tuned her out, focused on his own work.

Finn regarded her skeptically. "Care to share what that was about?"

"Elbridge Jewelers—well, someone who used to work there."

"How'd you get them to talk to you at two in the morning?"

"There's an ex-employee who got busted for pawning jewelry on the side. He's on parole, so all I had to do was reach out to his parole officer—Ed Buckley, he works the graveyard shift—and he was able to get through to him."

Finn nodded, impressed. "Go on. What'd you find?"

"Apparently these cuff links are high-end, custom-made. They're part of a limited edition set created by Elbridge Jewelers. Only ten were ever made."

"So our mystery man has money," Finn said.

"And has the initials TB."

"We have to narrow it down further," Finn murmured. "We can't exactly go through the phone book, looking up everyone with those initials."

The room lapsed into silence.

Finn snapped his fingers suddenly. "Wait a minute. Remember what Irene said at the bar? She thought the guy looked like a politician."

Sheila's eyes lit up. "You're right. That narrows it down considerably. Let's look into local politicians with the initials T.B."

Tapping away at his computer, Finn pulled up a list of current and former politicians in Coldwater County and the surrounding areas. The list was longer than they expected, a testament to the political engagement of their community.

"Timothy Barrow," Finn said, reading aloud. "He's on the school board."

Sheila shook her head. "Too old. Irene said the man looked to be in his forties or early fifties."

"Okay, how about Terry Benson? He's a state representative."

"No, he's been in Washington for the past month. Doesn't fit our timeline."

Finn continued scanning, unwilling to give up. "Tanner Briggs?" he suggested, stifling a yawn.

"The city comptroller? Possible, but he's not exactly known for his charisma. Doesn't seem like the type to lure women to their deaths." She paused. "What about Todd Blackwell?"

"He moved to Arizona last year. Remember the going-away party?"

She sighed, running a hand through her hair. "Maybe we're going about this the wrong way. He could be a former politician, or maybe someone who ran but didn't win. That could be part of their motive for—"

"Wait a minute," Finn said suddenly, sitting up straighter. He squinted at the screen. "Thomas Blake. How did we not think of him sooner?"

"The city councilman? What's so interesting about him?"

"Remember that campaign of his on the radio? The one about marriage?"

Sheila nodded slowly, her eyes glazing over with memory. "Vaguely."

"He's been pushing hard for stricter laws against adultery. Says it's 'destroying the fabric of our society.'"

Sheila leaned in, her excitement growing. "That fits. Both Laura and Sophie were involved in infidelity. What if Blake is targeting women he sees as threats to traditional marriage?"

"And that's not all. Guess where he regularly attends church?"

"St. Michael's?"

"St. Michael's."

CHAPTER EIGHT

The digital clock on the dashboard glowed 3:17 AM, its green numbers a stark contrast to the darkness enveloping Thomas Blake's property. Sheila shifted in her seat, trying to find a comfortable position in the confines of their unmarked police vehicle. Her eyes never left the sprawling Tudor-style house across the street, its windows dark and silent.

Finn sat beside her, his breathing steady and rhythmic. He was awake, she knew, but lost in his own thoughts. The silence between them was heavy with unspoken words and shared tension.

Sheila's mind wandered, as it often did during these long, quiet hours of surveillance. But her thoughts weren't on Thomas Blake. Instead, they kept circling back to Sophie Tournay's body, sprawled in that dirty alley like a broken doll.

The image was burned into her memory: Sophie's blonde hair matted with blood, her blue eyes staring sightlessly at the night sky. It was a sight that would haunt Sheila for a long time to come. But what troubled her even more was how vividly it had reminded her of another body, another tragic discovery.

Natalie.

She had felt the same way at the sight of Laura Hastings' body, but she'd managed to keep herself focused. Now, however, with space and time for her mind to roam, she felt the tug of the not-so-distant past.

She tried closing her eyes, but it didn't help. If anything, the darkness behind her eyelids only made the memories more vivid. She could see it all again, as clearly as if it were happening right now: walking into Natalie's cabin, calling out her sister's name…

And then finding her on the floor, unmoving, an empty pill bottle on the floor.

Sheila's hands clenched involuntarily, her nails digging into her palms. The pain was a welcome distraction from the memories threatening to overwhelm her.

Damn, I could use a drink, she thought.

Just one, to take the edge off. To dull the sharp edges of grief and guilt that still cut into her months after Natalie's death.

You made a promise to Finn, just as he made a promise to you. Neither of you drinks, ever. If you break that promise...

"You want to talk about her?" Finn asked.

Sheila glanced at him, puzzled. "Who?"

"Your sister."

"Is it that obvious?"

"That you're thinking about her? I'm sure you think about her all the time. So do I. She was a good friend."

Sheila gazed at Blake's house, lost in thought. *He knows me too well,* she thought, and for a moment she wondered if she'd made a mistake falling for him. After all, she couldn't lie to him the way she could lie to others. There was always a cost—to herself, if not to him.

He's good for you, she thought. *He's kind to you. And after what happened to Natalie, you need someone in your corner.*

"Tell me something positive," Finn said, oblivious to her thoughts. "Your best memory with her."

Sheila was quiet for a long moment, sifting through years of memories. Finally, she spoke. "There was this one time when we were kids. I must have been about eight, which would have made Natalie ten. Our parents had taken us camping up in the mountains."

She paused, a small smile tugging at her lips. "Natalie was always the brave one, you know? Always pushing boundaries. One night, she woke me up after our parents had gone to sleep. Said she wanted to go explore."

"In the middle of the night?" Finn asked, a note of amusement in his voice.

Sheila nodded. "Yeah. I was terrified, but I didn't want her to think I was a baby. So I went along. We snuck out of the tent and into the woods. It was so dark, I could barely see my hand in front of my face. But Natalie...she moved like she knew exactly where she was going."

"Where did she take you?"

"To this little clearing she'd found earlier in the day. When we got there, she told me to look up." Sheila's voice softened with the memory. "And when I did...Finn, I'd never seen so many stars in my life. It was like the whole universe was right there above us."

Finn smiled. "Sounds beautiful."

"It was. We lay there for hours, just staring up at the sky. Natalie knew all the constellations. She pointed them out to me, told me the stories behind them." Sheila's voice caught. "That's the Natalie I try to remember. Not...not how I found her."

Finn squeezed her hand. "The sister who showed you the stars. It's poetic."

Sheila nodded, blinking back tears. She felt suddenly grateful for Finn, but she didn't have the words to express it.

"What is it?" he asked softly.

She leaned closer, running a finger along his jawline...

Just then, a sudden flicker of light caught her attention. Her body tensed, instantly alert.

"Finn," she whispered, nodding toward Blake's house.

A light had come on in what appeared to be the kitchen. Through the gauzy curtains, they could see a figure moving around.

"It's three-thirty in the morning," Finn muttered. "What's he up to?"

They watched in tense silence as more lights came on in the house. The figure, presumably Blake, moved from room to room with purpose.

"He's getting dressed," Sheila said as the bedroom light flicked on. "Looks like he's in a hurry."

One by one, the lights winked off again until the only one remaining was on the ground floor, close to the front door. Then it went off, and the door opened. Thomas Blake emerged, dressed in a dark suit despite the early hour. He carried a briefcase and what looked like a small duffel bag.

"That doesn't look like someone heading out for an early meeting," Finn said, his voice low.

Blake hurried to his car, a sleek black sedan parked in the driveway. He threw his bags in the back seat and climbed in.

"He's running," Sheila said, her heart rate picking up. "Start the car, Finn. We can't lose him."

Finn turned the key in the ignition, the engine coming to life with a low rumble. They watched as Blake's car backed out of the driveway and started down the street.

"Lights off," Sheila said as Finn eased their vehicle onto the road. "We don't want to spook him."

They followed at a distance, keeping Blake's taillights in view but staying far enough back to avoid detection. The streets were empty at this hour, making it a delicate balance between not losing their target and not being too obvious.

Blake's car wound through the residential areas of Coldwater, eventually hitting the main road out of town.

"Where do you think he's headed?" Finn asked, his eyes never leaving the road.

Sheila shook her head. "I don't know, but wherever it is, he's in a hurry to get there."

Suddenly, Blake's car swerved sharply, cutting across two lanes of traffic.

"Damn it," Finn said, gripping the wheel tighter. "He's made us."

Sheila flicked on the siren and lights. "No point in hiding now. Stay with him!"

Blake's sedan accelerated, weaving dangerously between the few cars on the road. Finn matched his speed, the chase now in full swing.

"He's heading for the mountain road," Sheila said, her stomach tightening. The winding route was treacherous, even in broad daylight.

As they hit the first curve, Blake's car fishtailed, nearly clipping the guardrail. Finn's knuckles were white on the steering wheel, his face a mask of concentration as he navigated the hairpin turns.

"Sheila to dispatch," she barked into the radio. "We're in pursuit of a suspect on Mountain View Road. Suspect is Thomas Blake, driving a black sedan, license plate—"

Her words were cut off as Blake's car suddenly spun out, hitting the guardrail with a sickening crunch of metal. The sedan flipped, rolling once before coming to rest on its roof, smoke billowing from the engine.

Finn slammed on the brakes, bringing their vehicle to a screeching halt. They both leapt out, weapons drawn, approaching the wreckage cautiously.

"Blake!" Sheila called out. "Thomas Blake, can you hear me?"

There was no response. As they got closer, Sheila could see Blake hanging upside down, held in place by his seatbelt. He wasn't moving.

"Cover me," she told Finn, holstering her weapon and kneeling by the driver's side window. She reached in to check for a pulse.

"He's alive," she said. "Unconscious, but alive."

As Finn called for an ambulance, Sheila worked to extract Blake from the wreckage. Just as she managed to unbuckle his seatbelt and ease him onto the ground, his eyes fluttered open.

For a moment, Blake looked confused. Then his gaze focused on Sheila. "Please," he whispered, his tongue darting out to wet his lips. "Don't tell Leanna. Whatever happens…don't tell Leanna."

Sheila, confused, watched as Blake's eyes rolled back in his head and he lost consciousness again. Her gaze drifted to the sedan, where Finn was pulling out Blake's duffel bag. Finn set it on the ground and unzipped it.

"Sheila," he murmured in a strange voice.
"What?" she asked. "What is it?"
He turned it toward her, showing her the contents.
It was full of cash.

CHAPTER NINE

Sheila jolted awake, her heart racing as she felt someone shaking her shoulder. For a moment she was disoriented, the sterile white walls and antiseptic smell of the hospital room confusing her sleep-addled mind. The harsh fluorescent lights made her squint, and she could feel a crick in her neck from the awkward position she'd been sleeping in.

"Sheila," Finn said, his voice cutting through her fog. "Blake's out of surgery. He's awake."

She blinked, memories flooding back: the chase, the crash, the bag of cash. She hadn't meant to fall asleep, but exhaustion had finally caught up with her.

"What time is it?" she asked, her voice rough with sleep.

"Just after nine in the morning," Finn replied. "You've been out for a few hours. I tried to wake you earlier, but you were dead to the world."

Sheila stood, stretching out the kinks in her back from sleeping in the uncomfortable hospital chair. She ran a hand through her hair, trying to make herself presentable. "Any word from the station?"

Finn nodded. "They counted the cash: a hundred grand, even."

Sheila let out a low whistle. "That's a lot of green. Let's go figure out what he was planning to do with it."

As they approached Blake's room, a doctor stepped out to meet them. He was a middle-aged man with kind eyes and a neatly trimmed salt-and-pepper beard. "Deputies," he said, "I'm Dr. Angstrom. I've been overseeing Mr. Blake's care."

"How is he, doctor?" Sheila asked.

"Mr. Blake is stable, but he's suffered a concussion and several broken ribs. We're monitoring him closely for any signs of internal bleeding. The crash could have been much worse—he's lucky to be alive."

Sheila felt a mix of relief and frustration. They needed Blake alive to get answers, but his injuries meant they'd have to tread carefully in their questioning.

"Can we speak with him?" she asked.

"Yes, but please keep it brief," Dr. Angstrom said. "He needs rest, and too much stress could impede his recovery. If you notice any signs of distress—increased pain, shortness of breath, confusion—please alert the nursing staff immediately."

Sheila and Finn nodded their understanding. As they entered the room, Sheila's eyes were immediately drawn to the bed where Thomas Blake lay, looking pale and diminished against the white hospital sheets. His face was a patchwork of cuts and bruises, and an IV drip snaked into his arm. The steady beep of a heart monitor filled the room.

A woman sat beside him, her hand clasped tightly around his. She was in her early forties, with shoulder-length brown hair and the kind of polished appearance that screamed 'politician's wife.' She looked up as they entered, her eyes red-rimmed from crying.

"Mrs. Blake?" Sheila asked gently.

The woman nodded. "Leanna Blake. Are you the officers who...who found Thomas?"

Sheila's ears pricked up at the name. Leanna—the same name Blake had mentioned before losing consciousness. 'Don't tell Leanna,' he'd said. She exchanged a quick glance with Finn, seeing that he'd made the same connection.

"Yes, ma'am," Finn replied. "I'm Deputy Mercer, and this is Deputy Stone. We need to ask your husband a few questions about the accident. Would you mind giving us a moment alone with him?"

Leanna's grip on Blake's hand tightened. "I...I don't want to leave him. He's been through so much already."

"It's okay, honey," Blake said weakly. "I'll be fine. Just give us a few minutes."

Leanna looked torn, her eyes darting between her husband and the deputies. Finally, she nodded reluctantly. "Alright. But I'll be right outside if you need me, Thomas."

She stood and left the room, casting a worried glance back at her husband as she went. Sheila couldn't help but feel a pang of sympathy for the woman. Whatever was going on with Blake, it was clear his wife was caught in the middle of it.

Once the door closed behind Leanna, Sheila turned to Blake. His eyes were downcast, a mix of shame and fear evident on his face. The confident politician they'd seen in news clips and campaign posters was nowhere to be seen. In his place was a broken man, clearly wrestling with some inner turmoil.

Blake closed his eyes, a pained expression crossing his face. "I...I've made a terrible mistake," he whispered.

"What kind of mistake?" Finn asked.

Blake's eyes fluttered open, darting between Sheila and Finn. "I...I can't. You don't understand. If this gets out..."

"Mr. Blake," Sheila said, "we're not here to judge you. We're trying to solve a very serious crime. Anything you tell us could be crucial."

Blake shook his head slightly, wincing at the movement. "You don't get it. My career, my family...everything's at stake."

"Is this about Sophie Tournay?" Sheila asked.

Blake's eyes widened, fear flashing across his face. "How did you...? No, I can't talk about this."

Sheila took a deep breath, searching for the right words. "Thomas, whatever you're involved in, keeping silent will only make things worse. We need to know the truth."

Blake's gaze flickered, wavering. "It's not just about me," he muttered.

"Then who is it about? We can't help you if you don't open up."

Blake's eyes closed for a moment, as if gathering his strength. When he opened them again, there was a flicker of resolve. "Sophie and I...we were having an affair. But you probably know that already, don't you? Why else would you bring up her name?"

Sheila remained silent. Was it possible Blake didn't know about Sophie's death?

"How long has this affair been going on?" Finn asked.

"It started a few months ago," Blake said. "I knew Sophie had mixed feelings, knew she wasn't sure this was a good idea, but I never thought she'd go this far."

"Go this far?" Sheila asked, puzzled. "What are you talking about?"

"She texted me three nights ago, told me to meet her and bring one hundred thousand in cash—or else she'd go to the media, tell them everything. It wouldn't just ruin my career—my marriage would be over, too."

"What time did she text you?" Sheila asked.

"Must have been around…I don't know…ten o'clock? Maybe ten-thirty?"

Right after Sophie was seen leaving Chester's with that unidentified man, Sheila thought. Suddenly, it all made sense. Someone killed Sophie, then used her phone to blackmail Blake. But why? For the money, or as a way to get to Blake?

Sheila took a deep breath. "Mr. Blake, there's something you need to know. Sophie was murdered."

Blake's face went pale. "What? No, that can't be. What are you talking about?"

"I'm sorry," Sheila said softly. "The text wasn't from her. I believe someone killed Sophie and used her phone to blackmail you."

Blake looked stunned, his mind struggling to process the information. "But why? Why would someone do that?"

"We don't know yet," Sheila said.

"Where was this meeting supposed to happen?" Finn asked.

Blake took a moment to collect himself. "An old warehouse on the outskirts of town, near the abandoned railway tracks. She said to meet her there at four this morning."

CHAPTER TEN

Sheila and Finn stood outside the abandoned warehouse, its rusted metal exterior looming against the morning sky. The building was silent and unmoving against the bustling backdrop of the city behind it. A cool breeze rustled through the overgrown weeds surrounding the structure, carrying with it the faint scent of decay and neglect.

Sheila took a deep breath, trying to calm her nerves. She glanced at Finn, seeing the same mixture of anticipation and apprehension in his eyes that she felt herself.

"You ready?" Finn asked, his hand resting on his holstered weapon. His voice was steady, but Sheila could detect a hint of tension underneath.

She nodded, her jaw set with determination. "Let's do this."

They'd called for backup before arriving, a decision that now seemed prescient as they faced the imposing structure. Several patrol cars surrounded the perimeter, officers positioned at every exit. If anyone was inside, they weren't getting out unnoticed. The presence of their colleagues provided a small measure of comfort, but Sheila knew that ultimately, it would come down to her and Finn.

As they approached the main entrance, a large sliding door that had clearly seen better days, Sheila couldn't help but think about the events that had led them here. Blake's confession, Sophie's murder, the mysterious text message—it all seemed to converge on this desolate location.

The door groaned in protest as they forced it open, the sound violent in the quiet morning air. The interior was dim, shafts of sunlight filtering through dirty windows and holes in the roof, creating an eerie dance of light and shadow.

"CCSD! Anyone here?" Sheila called out, her voice echoing in the cavernous space. No response came, but the silence that followed seemed almost alive, pregnant with possibility.

The air was thick with dust and the musty smell of neglect, making her wish she had brought a mask. Every creak of the floorboards, every distant rustle, made her heart pound a little faster. She was acutely aware of her own breathing, loud in the stillness of the warehouse.

They moved cautiously through the space, flashlights sweeping across abandoned machinery and piles of debris. As Sheila's eyes adjusted to the dim light, she began to make out more details of their surroundings.

The warehouse appeared to have once been a textile factory. Large, rusted looms stood silent sentinel in neat rows, their intricate mechanisms frozen in time. Spools of thread, some still partially wound, lay scattered across workbenches and floors. In one corner, bolts of faded fabric leaned haphazardly against the wall, their patterns barely discernible under a thick layer of dust.

Overhead, a complex system of pulleys and conveyor belts crisscrossed the ceiling, testament to the efficient production line that once thrummed with activity here. Now cobwebs draped from the machinery like ghostly banners, swaying gently in the drafts that whispered through the dilapidated building.

As they delved deeper into the warehouse, the silence became oppressive. Sheila found herself straining to hear any sound that might indicate another presence, but there was nothing but the occasional groan of the building settling and their own cautious footsteps.

"Look at this," Finn said, his voice startlingly loud in the quiet. He was pointing to a cleared area near the center of the building. "Someone's been here recently."

Sheila examined the space, her flashlight beam cutting through the gloom. The floor was relatively clean, free from the layer of dust that covered everything else. In the center sat a folding chair and a small table, incongruous in their ordinariness amidst the abandoned industrial setting.

She tried to imagine Blake standing here, a duffel bag of money in his hand, his heart probably racing as fast as hers was now. What had he been thinking? If he had made it here on time, would he ever have made it out alive?

"This must be where the killer planned to meet Blake," she said.

"And then what?" Finn asked, voicing the question that was on both their minds. "At that point, he can't just let him go."

Sheila shrugged. "Then he kills Blake."

"Why? To cover his tracks? Or does he really need the money?"

Sheila was about to answer when she noticed something: an object hanging from a nail tacked to a corkboard.

A rosary, its beads worn and the crucifix slightly tarnished.

"He was here, alright," Sheila murmured. "And I think he wants us to know it."

***

"So we've got two women murdered by a man posing as a priest, and a rosary left at a warehouse where a politician who was being blackmailed was supposed to drop off one hundred grand in cash. Am I tracking so far?"

Hank Dawson, Coldwater County's interim sheriff after the death of Natalie, leaned back in his chair and regarded Sheila and Finn with a thoughtful frown. He was a stout man with a neatly trimmed mustache that failed to disguise his cherubic face.

"That's about right," Sheila said.

"What are we dealing with, then? Some kind of religious fanatic?"

"We're not sure," Finn said. "Could be punishing the victims for infidelity. Maybe someone in his life cheated on him, and now he's on a crusade to punish others."

Hank sighed, rubbing his temples. "I don't like this, not one bit. A killer with a possible religious motive...that's gonna stir up all kinds of trouble in the community."

He stood up, pacing behind his desk. "You two have no idea the kind of pressure I'm under. The mayor's breathing down my neck, demanding results. The press is circling like vultures, and now everything with Thomas Blake…" He shook his head woefully. "There's no keeping this under wraps now."

Sheila could see the worry in Hank's eyes. He was a good man, dedicated to the town, but she knew he was out of his depth with a case like this. She felt a pang of sympathy for him, thrust into a role he hadn't asked for and wasn't fully prepared to handle.

"Any idea whether this guy's really a priest?" Hank asked.

"There's something else, sir," she said, her voice grave. "We learned from the bartender at Chester's that Sophie left with a man claiming to be a priest. We don't know if it's connected, but..."

"Not yet," Finn said. "But given that no one at St. Michael's seems to know about him, we have to consider the possibility that it's just a ruse."

Hank collapsed back into his chair. "This just keeps getting better and better. What's your next move?"

Sheila exchanged a glance with her partner before answering. "We think it might be worth talking to Father Stephen again, see if he knows anybody by the name of Wayland."

"Wayland?"

"According to James Hastings," Finn said, "that's the name of the priest his wife was meeting with."

Hank nodded slowly. "Alright, that sounds like a good plan. But tread carefully, you two. We don't want to cause a panic or start pointing fingers at the religious community without solid evidence."

"Understood, sir," Sheila said.

Hank sighed, running a hand through his thinning hair. "And keep me in the loop. I need to know everything that's happening, no matter how small it might seem. We can't afford any surprises, not with this case."

Sheila and Finn nodded and left the office, both lost in thought as they made their way through the station. The buzz of activity around them seemed distant to Sheila, muffled by the gravity of their task.

As they stepped outside the police station, they were immediately bombarded by a group of reporters who had been lying in wait.

"Deputy Stone! Deputy Mercer!" A young woman with a microphone thrust it toward them. "Is it true that the 'Coldwater Confessor' has struck again?"

Sheila blinked, taken aback. "I'm sorry, the what?"

"The Coldwater Confessor," another reporter said. "That's what people are calling the killer. Is it true he's targeting sinners? Is this a religiously motivated series of murders?"

Finn cleared his throat. "We're in the midst of an ongoing investigation and can't comment on specifics. We urge the public to remain calm and report any suspicious activity to the police."

"But Deputy," a third reporter pressed, "sources say you found religious artifacts at the latest crime scene. Can you confirm this?"

Sheila felt a surge of frustration. How had that information leaked? "As my partner said, we can't comment on an active investigation. Now, if you'll excuse us..."

They pushed their way through the crowd, reporters still shouting questions at their backs. When they finally reached their vehicle, Sheila slumped against the door, exhaling heavily.

"'Coldwater Confessor'?" she muttered. "Great. Just what we need: a catchy name to whip everyone into a frenzy."

Finn nodded grimly as he unlocked the car. "You know how it goes: The press loves a good serial killer story. We'd better solve this fast, because if we don't...this town is going to eat itself alive."

CHAPTER ELEVEN

Rachel Kim burst through the front door of her Coldwater mansion, her stilettos clicking angrily against the polished marble floor of her foyer.

"Mochi?" she called out, her voice tinged with frustration. "Where are you, you little furball?"

No answering yap came in response, which was unusual. Mochi, her beloved Shih Tzu, always greeted her at the door with excited barks and wagging tail. But today, the house remained oddly quiet.

Rachel sighed, dropping her designer handbag on the antique side table by the door. This day was turning into a complete disaster. First, her dog-sitter had called out at the last minute, forcing her to rush home in the middle of the workday to let Mochi out. Now, she was going to miss the most important meeting of her career so far.

As the youngest executive at Elbridge Tech, Rachel had worked tirelessly to prove herself. At twenty-six, she'd already climbed the corporate ladder faster than anyone else in the company's history. But she knew that in the cutthroat world of tech startups, you were only as good as your last success.

Today's meeting was with a group of potential investors from Silicon Valley. If she could secure their funding, it would catapult Elbridge Tech into the big leagues. More importantly, it would cement her position as a rising star in the industry.

But now, because of her irresponsible dog-sitter and her own soft spot for her furry companion, she was going to miss it.

Why didn't I just let him pee on the rug? She thought. *It wouldn't be the first time he's done it.*

But she knew the reason. Mochi didn't like peeing in the house, and so he would hold it as long as he could—which was how he'd developed a UTI and then a near-fatal kidney infection just last year. Rachel cared too much for the little furball to risk that happening again.

Her thoughts drifted to the day she'd gotten Mochi. It had been just after her grandmother's funeral three years ago. She'd been devastated by her grandmother's death, feeling alone in a world that suddenly seemed much colder. Her parents, ever practical, had suggested she focus on her career to distract herself from the grief. But Rachel had needed something more.

She'd found Mochi at a local shelter, a tiny ball of fluff with soulful eyes that seemed to see right through her carefully constructed façade of strength. In that moment, she'd known she needed this little dog as much as he needed her.

Since then, Mochi had been her constant companion, her confidant, and her anchor in the stormy seas of her high-pressure life. He was the one being she could be completely herself around, without fear of judgment or expectations.

"Mochi?" Rachel called again, a note of worry creeping into her voice. She moved further into the house, her heels now sinking into the plush carpet of the living room. "Come on, boy. Where are you hiding?"

She checked all of Mochi's favorite spots: under the coffee table, behind the couch, in the laundry room where he liked to curl up in warm piles of clothes. But there was no sign of him anywhere.

A cold knot of fear began to form in Rachel's stomach. Had Mochi somehow gotten out? But how? The house was secure, with top-of-the-line locks and an expensive security system. She'd made sure of that after reading about a series of break-ins in the neighborhood last year.

Just as she was about to call the local animal control, a knock at the door startled her. Rachel hesitated, her hand hovering over her phone. Who could that be? She wasn't expecting anyone, and solicitors rarely made it past the gated community's security.

If it's one of those nutjobs handing out pamphlets again...

Another knock, more insistent this time. Rachel smoothed her skirt and made her way back to the foyer. Through the frosted glass panels flanking the door, she could make out the silhouette of a man.

What was that in his arms?

Taking a deep breath, Rachel opened the door. There, on her doorstep, stood a middle-aged man with salt-and-pepper hair and kind eyes. In his arms was a familiar ball of fluff.

"Mochi!" Rachel exclaimed, relief flooding through her.

The man smiled, holding out the squirming dog. "I believe this little fellow belongs to you?"

Rachel scooped Mochi into her arms, hugging him tight. "Yes, yes he does. Oh, thank you so much! Where did you find him?"

"He was wandering down Maple Street, looking quite lost," the man said. "Luckily, one of the neighbors recognized him. I'm Jack, by the way. I live a few blocks over on Elm."

Rachel nodded—he *did* look vaguely familiar. "I'm Rachel. I can't thank you enough, Jack. I was so worried when I couldn't find him."

Jack waved off her thanks. "It was no trouble at all. I'm just glad I could reunite you two." He paused, looking slightly embarrassed. "I hate to impose, but would you mind if I washed my hands? My wife is terribly allergic to dogs, and I'd rather not bring any fur home with me."

Rachel hesitated. She generally didn't like letting strangers into her home, but this man had just done her an enormous favor. It seemed ungrateful to refuse such a simple request.

"Of course," she said, stepping back to allow him entry. "The powder room is just down the hall, first door on the left."

Jack smiled gratefully and stepped inside. Rachel closed the door behind him, still cuddling Mochi close. She'd have to figure out how he'd gotten out later. For now, she was just relieved to have him back safe and sound.

As Jack disappeared down the hallway, Rachel set Mochi down and grabbed her phone. She fired off a quick text to her assistant, explaining the situation and asking her to reschedule the investor meeting if possible. It was a long shot, but maybe she could still salvage this day.

She was just setting the phone down on a table when a voice from behind her startled her. "You have a lovely home," Jack said. She hadn't heard him return.

"Oh, thank you," Rachel replied, turning to face him. "I've put a lot of work into it."

Jack nodded, his eyes roaming over the expensive furnishings and artwork. "I can see that. It's quite...impressive."

There was something in his tone that made Rachel uneasy. It wasn't quite disapproval, but it wasn't admiration either. She suddenly felt the urge to defend herself, though she wasn't sure why.

"I've worked hard to get where I am," she said, her chin lifting slightly.

Jack's eyes snapped back to her, a strange intensity in his gaze. "I'm sure you have. But tell me, Rachel, do you ever feel like something's missing? Like all of this," he gestured around the room, "isn't quite enough?"

Rachel blinked, taken aback by the personal nature of the question. "I...I'm not sure what you mean."

Jack took a step closer, and Rachel instinctively took one back. "I mean, do you ever feel an emptiness in your life? A longing for something more...spiritual?"

Alarm bells began to ring in Rachel's head. This conversation had taken a bizarre turn, and she was starting to feel very uncomfortable.

"I'm an atheist, actually," she said, hoping to shut down this line of questioning. "I don't really believe in anything spiritual."

Jack's face darkened, and Rachel resisted the urge to shudder. "That's a shame," he said, his voice low and intense. "A young woman like you, wallowing in the darkness of your own disbelief. It's not too late to save your soul, you know."

Rachel's heart began to race. This wasn't right. Something was very, very wrong. She needed to get this man out of her house now.

"I think you should leave," she said, trying to keep her voice steady. "Thank you again for bringing Mochi back, but I have a lot of work to do."

Jack didn't move. Instead, his eyes seemed to bore into her, filled with a fervor that frightened her. "I can't leave you like this, Rachel. You need to be shown the error of your ways. You need to be cleansed. Join me and I will show you the truth."

Rachel's blood ran cold. Join him? What in the world was he talking about? Her mind flashed to the news reports she'd been seeing lately, about a killer targeting women in Coldwater. Could it be...?

She needed to call for help. Her phone was on the side table, just a few feet away. If she could just reach it...

"I...I appreciate your concern," she said, forcing a smile as she picked up her phone again, trying to act casual about it. "But really, I'm fine. I'm happy with my life as it is."

Jack shook his head sadly. "No, you're not. You're lost, Rachel. Only I can help you—nobody else."

She pretended not to have heard him. "The whole company seems to fall apart as soon as I'm gone," she said with a nervous laugh, tapping away at the phone as if sending a text to a colleague. Instead, however, she dialed 9-1-1.

Keep him talking, she thought. *Keep him distracted.*

"Do you have a job, Jack?" she asked, glancing up from her phone. Then she froze in horror. Jack was now holding an ornate brass candlestick—one she recognized from her own dining room.

Jack raised the candlestick, a serene smile on his face that contrasted horrifically with the violence of his posture. "I gave you a chance, Rachel, but you refused. This is on you."

Rachel screamed as Jack lunged forward, the candlestick arcing through the air toward her head. She ducked, feeling the rush of air as it narrowly missed her. Mochi was barking frantically, adding to the chaos.

She scrambled away, her heels slipping on the polished floor. Jack pursued her, his face twisted into a mask of righteous fury. Rachel's mind raced, searching for a way out. The front door was blocked. The back door was too far. She needed a weapon, something to defend herself with.

As she rounded the kitchen island, her hand closed around the handle of a heavy cast iron skillet. Without thinking, she swung it with all her might.

Jack raised his arm, and the pan collided with his elbow, ringing hollowly. He let out an angry cry. Rachel dropped the skillet and ran for the front door, Mochi at her heels.

She was opening the door when something struck her from behind. There was no pain—just a flash of light and a strange numbness. Then she was falling, falling to the tiled floor, and the last thing she knew was the softness of Mochi's tongue on her cheek.

CHAPTER TWELVE

Father Stephen was lighting candles at the altar when Sheila and Finn entered St. Michael's Church. The soft glow of the flames cast dancing shadows across the ornate stained glass windows, creating an atmosphere of reverence and solemnity. The scent of incense lingered in the air, a reminder of the morning's mass.

"Father Stephen," Sheila called out softly, not wanting to startle the priest.

He turned, a warm smile spreading across his face as he recognized them. "Deputies Stone and Mercer. What brings you back to our humble church?"

As they approached, Sheila noticed the dark circles under Father Stephen's eyes. The strain of recent events was clearly taking its toll on him.

"We have some questions about the case, Father," Finn said. "We were hoping you might be able to help us."

Father Stephen nodded, gesturing for them to sit in the front pew. "Of course. I'll help in any way I can. These tragedies have shaken our community to its core."

As they settled into the hard wooden seats, Sheila pulled out her notebook. "Father, we've come across a name in our investigation. Does the name Father Wayland mean anything to you?"

The priest furrowed his brow, thinking for a moment. "Father Wayland? No, I'm afraid that doesn't ring any bells. Is he connected to the case somehow?"

Sheila exchanged a glance with Finn before answering. "We're not sure yet. But it seems that Laura Hastings may have met with a priest calling himself Father Wayland shortly before her death, and we have reason to believe Sophie Tournay met with the same person."

Father Stephen's eyes widened. "Oh, my. Yes, I heard about poor Ms. Tournay on the news. That's...concerning. But I can assure you, there's no Father Wayland associated with this church or any in the diocese that I'm aware of."

"What about new priests or visiting clergy?" Finn asked. "Anyone who might have been here temporarily?"

Father Stephen shook his head. "No, we haven't had any visitors recently. It's just been me for the past few months." He paused, a troubled look crossing his face. "Although..."

"Yes?" Sheila leaned forward, sensing they might be on the verge of a breakthrough.

"Well, it's probably nothing," Father Stephen said hesitantly. "But about a month ago, I noticed a few things missing from the vestry: candlesticks, robes. I assumed I'd simply misplaced them, but now..."

Sheila's mind was already racing with the implications. "Father, we're going to need a list of everyone who has access to the vestry."

"Of course," Father Stephen said, his voice heavy with worry. "I hope you catch this person. I can't stand to think that our church might have inadvertently played a role in these horrible crimes."

Sheila placed a comforting hand on his arm. "This isn't your fault, Father. You're helping us catch the real culprit."

He nodded, but he still looked troubled. "I'll be praying you succeed."

As the priest moved away, Finn turned to Sheila. "This could be our break," he said. "If our killer is impersonating a priest, it explains how he's gaining his victims' trust."

Sheila nodded, but her brow was furrowed. "But it also means he could be anyone. We're not just looking for a rogue priest anymore—we're looking for someone with enough knowledge of the church to convincingly play the part. That's a big group."

As they were preparing to leave, an elderly woman walked past them, her wizened face creased with concern as she approached the priest. "Father Stephen, I just wanted to say how sorry I am about poor Laura. Such a tragedy."

Sheila's ears perked up at the mention of Laura's name. She was about to introduce herself when Finn's phone buzzed. He excused himself to take the call, stepping away to the back of the church.

"I'm Deputy Stone," Sheila said, turning to the old woman.

"Francine Albright."

"Did you know Laura Hastings well, Ms. Albright?"

The woman nodded, her eyes misting over. "Oh yes, dear. I'm here most days, you see. Laura was such a sweet girl, always had a kind word for everyone."

Sheila's investigator instincts kicked in. If this woman was at the church frequently, she might have noticed something others had missed. "You're here often, then? Have you noticed anything unusual lately? Any strangers or new faces?"

The old woman thought for a moment, her gnarled hands fidgeting with her rosary beads. "Well, now that you mention it, I did see a priest I didn't recognize a few weeks back. Thought it was odd, as Father Stephen hadn't mentioned any visitors."

Sheila's heart rate quickened. "Can you describe him?"

"Oh, let me think," Francine said, her brow furrowing in concentration. "He was tall, I remember that. Gray hair, very neat. And he had the kindest eyes, like he could see right into your soul. But there was something...intense about him, too. Made me a bit uncomfortable, if I'm being honest."

"Did you speak with him?" Sheila asked, trying to keep the excitement out of her voice.

The old woman nodded slowly. "Just briefly. He asked about confession times, said he was new in town. I directed him to Father Stephen, but..." She trailed off, looking troubled.

"But what?" Sheila encouraged gently.

"He never spoke with me," Father Stephen said.

"I assumed I'd just misunderstood something," the old woman answered.

Sheila was about to ask more questions when Finn returned, his face grim. "Sheila, we need to go. Now."

"What is it?" she asked, sensing the urgency in his tone.

Finn lowered his voice. "There's been another murder. A woman killed in her own home. They think it might be connected to our case."

***

The Kim residence was a hive of activity when Sheila and Finn arrived. Crime scene technicians in white suits moved methodically through the expansive foyer, photographing and cataloging evidence. The air was thick with tension and the metallic scent of blood.

As they stepped inside, Sheila immediately noticed the stark contrast between the opulent surroundings and the brutal crime scene. Crystal chandeliers cast a soft glow over marble floors, now marred by bloody footprints. It was a jarring juxtaposition of wealth and violence.

Dr. Jin Zihao was crouched over a body near the base of a grand staircase. As Sheila and Finn approached, he looked up, his face grim.

"Deputies," he said by way of greeting. "I wish we were meeting under better circumstances."

Sheila nodded, her eyes fixed on the victim. Rachel Kim lay sprawled on the marble floor, her business attire now stained crimson. The young woman's face was barely recognizable, battered beyond recognition.

She was petite, probably no taller than 5'2", with a slender build that spoke of regular workouts and a carefully maintained diet. Her black hair, now matted with blood, was cut in a sleek bob that framed her face, a style that projected professionalism and sophistication. Even in death, her nails were perfectly manicured, painted a subtle nude shade that complemented her olive skin tone.

She wore a tailored charcoal gray suit, the jacket now askew and stained crimson. The outfit was clearly expensive, possibly designer, indicating a woman who valued appearance and had the means to maintain it. A delicate gold necklace with a small diamond pendant lay at her throat, twisted in the struggle but still catching the light.

Despite the damage inflicted by the attack, Sheila could see that Rachel had been an attractive woman, with high cheekbones and full lips. Her eyes, though now lifeless, were almond-shaped, hinting at her Korean heritage.

"She was clearly successful," Finn murmured, taking in the details of Rachel's appearance and her opulent surroundings. "Young, wealthy, probably at the top of her game."

Sheila nodded, a lump forming in her throat. "And now she's another victim. Is the cause of death as obvious as it appears?"

Dr. Zihao gestured to a blood-stained candlestick lying a few feet from the body. "Blunt force trauma to the head. Multiple strikes. The killer was...thorough."

Sheila felt a chill run down her spine. "Just like Laura Hastings and Sophie Tournay."

"Yes," Dr. Zihao said. "The wounds are consistent with the other victims. I'd stake my reputation on this being the work of your Coldwater Confessor."

Sheila turned and peered through the doorway, studying the front door. "No signs of forced entry," she murmured. "So either Rachel knew her killer, or..."

"Or he somehow gained her trust enough to let him in," Finn said.

They exchanged a troubled look. This new detail added another layer of complexity to an already puzzling case.

Just then, a commotion outside caught Sheila's attention. She stepped outside to see a middle-aged man arguing with an officer.

"Please," he said, trying to get to the front door. "I just need to speak with someone in charge." His eyes met Sheila's, pleading for her understanding.

"Let him through," Sheila said.

The officer, a burly man with sideburns, grunted and stepped aside.

"I'm Deputy Stone," Sheila said as the man approached. "And you are?"

"David Larson," he replied, his face etched with worry. "I live next door. Is it true? About Rachel?"

Sheila exchanged a glance with Finn, who was now standing behind her, before responding. "Mr. Larson, I'm afraid Rachel Kim has been killed. We're investigating it now. Did you know her well?"

David ran a hand through his thinning hair, visibly shaken. "We weren't close, but we've been neighbors for three years. She was...she was a good person. Driven, you know? Always working."

"Can you tell us more about her?" Finn asked. "Anything you know could be helpful."

David nodded, collecting his thoughts. "She worked at Elbridge Tech, some big executive position. Always left early, came home late. Lived for her job, I think."

"Was she religious at all?" Sheila asked. "Did you ever see her attend church or anything like that?"

To their surprise, David let out a short, humorless laugh. "Rachel? Religious? No way. She was about as atheistic as they come. I remember she hosted a winter solstice party last year instead of Christmas. Said she preferred to celebrate science over superstition."

Sheila and Finn exchanged a startled glance. This revelation threw their entire theory into disarray. If Rachel wasn't religious, why had the killer targeted her?

"Are you sure?" Sheila asked. "She never mentioned meeting with a priest or seeking spiritual guidance?"

"Absolutely not," David said. "Rachel was all about facts and logic. She thought religion was...well, let's just say she wasn't a fan."

"What about her personal life?" Finn asked. "Did she have many visitors? A boyfriend or girlfriend, perhaps?"

David shook his head. "Not that I ever saw. Like I said, she was always working. The only regular visitor I ever noticed was her dog walker."

Sheila glanced at Finn, who in turn addressed the burly officer. "Hey, Chad, you hear anything about a dog?"

"Yeah, there was one hiding in the bedroom," he said. "Animal control picked him up already."

Sheila turned her attention back to David. "So this dog walker would've had access to the house?" she asked.

David nodded. "That's right."

"You wouldn't know where we can find him by any chance, would you?"

CHAPTER THIRTEEN

"I can't tell whether we're on to something," Sheila said as she drove, "or if we're going deeper down the rabbit hole."

Sheila and Finn were on their way to speak with Jason Reeves, Rachel Kim's twenty-eight-year-old dog walker. He'd been working as a professional dog walker for the past five years with several clients in Rachel's upscale neighborhood. He had no criminal record and no religious affiliations that might make him a more likely suspect.

"I know. But we have to follow every lead, no matter how small," Finn said, studying his phone. "This guy had access to Rachel's house—we can't just ignore that."

Sheila said nothing. She sensed they were missing little details—details that might be the difference between life and death for the killer's next target.

Jason's modest apartment building was older, clad in a faded brick exterior crawling with rusted fire escapes. A few kids were playing in the small courtyard, their laughter echoing off the walls.

Sheila parked the car, and the two of them got out. They entered the building and climbed the creaking stairs to the third floor, the smell of various lunches cooking wafting through the hallways. Finn knocked on the door of apartment 3B, the sound echoing in the narrow corridor. There was no response.

"Lights are on," Finn murmured. "So why isn't he answering?"

Sheila was about to knock when she heard it: a muffled coughing sound coming from within the apartment. Her pulse quickened. Was Jason trying to hide from them? Or was something else going on?

"Jason Reeves?" Sheila called. "This is the police. We'd like to speak with you about Rachel Kim."

"Come in!" came a choked voice, followed by more coughing.

Finn tried the door handle, finding it unlocked. They entered cautiously, sweeping the small living room with their eyes. The apartment was cluttered but not dirty, with dog-themed decor scattered about. A half-eaten bowl of soup sat on the coffee table, still steaming.

And there, sprawled on a worn couch, was Jason Reeves. He looked pale and sickly, his face shiny with sweat. The apartment smelled of illness and disinfectant, making Sheila wrinkle her nose.

"Mr. Reeves?" Finn asked. "We'd like to ask you some questions about Rachel Kim."

Jason groaned, sitting up slowly. His movements were weak and uncoordinated. "Rachel?" he croaked, his voice hoarse. "Is she okay? I had to cancel on her this morning. Food poisoning hit me hard last night."

Sheila and Finn looked at one another. If Jason had been here, sick, all day, he couldn't have been involved in Rachel's murder. Assuming he wasn't faking his condition, of course. They still needed to establish an alibi, though—they couldn't just take his word for it.

"How long have you been ill, exactly?" Sheila asked.

Jason reached for a glass of water on the coffee table, his hand shaking slightly. "Since about ten last night," he replied after taking a sip. "Bad takeout, I think. From that new place on fifth. I've been stuck here ever since. Called all my clients first thing this morning to cancel."

"Can you prove that?" Finn asked.

Jason nodded weakly, reaching for his phone. "Yeah, check my call logs. And I've got the takeout receipt somewhere...probably in the kitchen."

"Can anyone verify that you've been here?" Sheila asked as Finn left to find the receipt.

Jason frowned, thinking. "My neighbor, Mrs. Goldstein in 3A, she brought me some ginger tea this morning. And the delivery guy who brought my meds saw me, too. You can check with them."

Sheila nodded, making a mental note. "We'll do that. Mind telling me when the last time you saw Rachel Kim was?"

"Would've been...two days ago? Yeah, Tuesday afternoon. I walked Mochi—that's her dog—while she was at work. I saw her right before she left."

"Did you notice anything unusual? Anyone hanging around her house, maybe?"

Jason shook his head, then winced at the movement. "No, nothing out of the ordinary. Rachel's neighborhood is pretty quiet. Lots of security systems, you know?"

Finn returned with the takeout receipt, confirming Jason's story.

As Sheila's eyes scanned the room, they landed on the half-eaten bowl of soup on the coffee table. Something about it caught her attention. She leaned in closer, careful not to touch anything.

"Mr. Reeves," she asked, "is this the takeout that made you sick?"

Jason nodded weakly. "That's right. Why?"

Sheila peered into the bowl, her brow furrowing. Nothing about the soup looked strange...still, Sheila had a nagging suspicion that something was wrong here.

"Mind if we take this?" she asked.

Jason's eyes narrowed, and he blinked at her, puzzled. "Uh...yeah, sure, I guess."

"Thank you." Sheila snapped the lid back over the styrofoam soup bowl, then picked it up. "We appreciate your time, Mr. Reeves, and we hope you feel better soon. Let us know if you think of anything else."

As they left Jason's apartment, Finn turned to Sheila. "What's with the soup? You think there's something off about it?"

Sheila nodded, her expression grim. "I have a hunch it might be poisoned. Think about it—if Jason was too sick to walk Rachel's dog, she'd have to come home early to take care of Mochi herself."

"Assuming she didn't have anyone else she could call," Finn said. "And that's a big assumption."

He had a point. Still, Sheila was undeterred.

"Maybe the killer knew her well enough to know she wouldn't let just anyone walk her dog," she said. "Either way, it seems like just the sort of devious thing our killer would do. He poses as a priest, he kills one woman in a confessional and lures another into an alley..."

"He's clever, that's for sure."

Sheila nodded. "And that's why I want to take this to the lab. Because if we just focus on the big break, the obvious explanation...we might never catch this guy."

***

This place is a jungle, Sheila thought, gazing around in surprise.

The forensics lab was located in the basement of the Coldwater County Sheriff's Department. Ordinarily the lab, all gleaming stainless steel and state-of-the-art equipment, was fairly quiet, humming with efficiency. Today, however, the lab seemed particularly chaotic.

On the drive here from Jason Reeves' apartment, Dawson had called for an update and explained that the Coldwater Confessor case had exploded in the media, because of which the mayor had ordered a review of all unsolved homicides from the past five years, looking for any possible links to the current case. This meant that boxes of old evidence had been dragged out of storage, filling every available surface in the lab.

Adding to the mayhem, a local reporter had leaked information about DNA evidence found at one of the crime scenes. This had led to a flood of calls from concerned citizens, each claiming to have information about suspicious individuals who might match the DNA profile. The lab was now processing hundreds of voluntary DNA samples, trying to rule out potential suspects.

Amidst all this, the regular caseload of the department hadn't decreased. If anything, the general sense of unease in Coldwater had led to an uptick in reported crimes, each requiring its own set of forensic analyses.

Sheila and Finn had to weave their way through a maze of busy technicians and towering stacks of evidence boxes to reach Dr. Patel, the head forensic analyst. Despite the chaos around him, Dr. Patel stood out like a calm eye in the storm. He was a tall, lean man in his fifties, with skin the color of polished mahogany and a shock of prematurely white hair that seemed to defy gravity. His most striking feature, however, was his eyes: heterochromatic, one a deep brown and the other a startling blue. These mismatched eyes peered out from behind thick-rimmed glasses, giving him an air of both eccentricity and intense focus.

Dr. Patel was hunched over a microscope, his lab coat rumpled and his tie askew. A half-empty cup of cold coffee sat precariously close to the edge of his workstation. He barely looked up as they approached, his mismatched eyes fixed intently on whatever sample he was examining.

"Dr. Patel," Sheila began, "we need your help with—"

"Let me guess," he said, finally turning to face them. "Another rush job?"

Finn nodded. "We have a soup sample we need tested for poison. It could be crucial to—"

Dr. Patel held up a hand, stopping Finn mid-sentence. "I'm sorry, deputies, but we're swamped here. The mayor's pushing for results on three different high-profile cases, not to mention the backlog from last month's evidence room flood. I simply don't have the manpower or the time to add another test to our workload right now."

Sheila felt her frustration rising. "This isn't some decades-old unsolved homicide. This is the Coldwater Confessor case, an active serial killer investigation."

Dr. Patel blinked at her as if a light had just gone on in his head. "Of course," he murmured. "I'll run a test right away. But I have to warn you: This test will only detect a limited number of common toxins—it won't give us a comprehensive analysis. So don't get your hopes up."

"Thank you, Dr. Patel," Sheila said, relieved.

"Alright then," Dr. Patel said. "Let's see what your mysterious soup has to tell us."

He gestured for them to follow him to a less crowded corner of the lab, where he donned a fresh pair of gloves and carefully opened the soup container.

He dipped the paper strip into the soup, then placed it on a small device that looked like a cross between a scanner and a spectrometer. The machine hummed to life, and a series of numbers and graphs appeared on its attached screen.

As they waited for the results, Sheila couldn't help but ask, "Dr. Patel, how did you end up in forensics? It seems like a...unique career choice."

The scientist's lips quirked in a small smile. "I was pre-med in college, but I found I preferred working with the dead more than the living. Less complaining."

Before Sheila could respond to this rather morbid joke, the machine beeped. Dr. Patel leaned in, scanning the results rapidly.

"Well, I'll be damned," he muttered.

"What is it?" Sheila asked, leaning forward.

Dr. Patel turned to face her, his expression grave. "Your hunch was right, deputy. This soup contains significant traces of ipecac syrup—an emetic agent used to induce vomiting."

CHAPTER FOURTEEN

The Father sat in his dim living room, the afternoon sun barely penetrating the heavy curtains. His eyes were fixed on the television screen, where Samantha Chen, Coldwater's most prominent news anchor, was delivering the latest update on the case. Her sleek black hair and crisp blue blazer were immaculate, perfectly arranged.

"...and police are still searching for leads in the case of the so-called 'Coldwater Confessor'," she was saying, her voice carrying just a hint of tension beneath its professional veneer. "Sources close to the investigation suggest that the killer may be targeting individuals based on perceived moral transgressions. However, the recent murder of Rachel Kim, a known atheist, has thrown this theory into question."

The Father leaned forward, interested. They knew more than he'd anticipated. The police were proving to be more capable than he'd given them credit for.

Samantha continued, her dark eyes looking directly into the camera. "Sheriff Dawson had this to say at this morning's press conference."

The screen cut to footage of Sheriff Dawson, his face set in determination as he addressed a crowd of reporters. "We are pursuing all leads and will not rest until this killer is brought to justice. We urge the public to remain vigilant and report any suspicious activity immediately."

The Father allowed himself a small smile at the moniker they'd given him. They really had no idea why he was doing all this, did they?

He hadn't planned for these cleansings to become so public, to garner such attention. He was simply fulfilling his mission, not looking for acclaim. Still...there had to be a way to leverage the situation, didn't there?

The Father stood, pacing the room as his mind blossomed with possibilities. This platform, this attention—it was an opportunity. A chance to spread his message further, to make more people understand the importance of his work.

Yes, he decided, nodding to himself. It was time to take control of the narrative. To show them all the true purpose behind his actions.

He moved to his desk, opening a drawer and carefully removing an object. It was a vintage ink stamp, its handle worn smooth with age. The stamp itself was in the shape of a crucifix surrounded by a halo of thorns.

The Father held the stamp up to the light, admiring its craftsmanship. Yes, this would do just nicely. This would prove his identity—

And let everyone know he wasn't going to hide in the shadows. He had a message for the world...and he was going to tell it using the biggest microphone possible.

Death itself.

CHAPTER FIFTEEN

Sheila stared at the whiteboard in the conference room, her eyes tracing the connections between the victims' photos. The faces of Laura Hastings, Sophie Tournay, and Rachel Kim looked back at her, smiling in blissful ignorance of the fate awaiting them.

"Okay, let's go over this one more time," Sheila said, turning to Finn, who was nursing his third cup of coffee. The lack of sleep the previous night and the intensity of their investigation were taking their toll on both of them.

Finn nodded, setting down his mug. "We believe the killer poisoned Jason Reeves to ensure Rachel Kim would be home."

"Right," Sheila said. "But we're still no closer to figuring out how the killer managed to poison Jason's takeout."

Finn sighed, rubbing his temples. "I know. We checked every angle. The restaurant's clean—all employees accounted for, no suspicious temp workers. The delivery service, too. We even got the security camera footage, but there was nothing out of the ordinary."

"And Jason swears he didn't leave the food unattended at any point," Sheila added. "It's like the poison just appeared out of thin air."

"There *was* that one manager who mentioned a surprise visit by a health inspector. Could that have been the killer?"

Sheila shrugged. "Possibly. No camera footage, though, no name or other identification, nothing more than a vague description: 'good-looking and of average height.' Not very helpful."

They were both silent for several moments.

"I know it's frustrating," Sheila said, "but we have to face facts—we don't know how the killer poisoned Jason's food. So for now, let's move on to the next thing we know."

Finn cleared his throat. "Alright. We believe the killer convinced Laura that he was a priest named Father Wayland, and probably did the same with Sophie."

"Right," Sheila said. "And he killed each of them with a blunt object—a candlestick with Laura and Rachel, and possibly the same with Sophie. But why these women? What's the connection?"

"It can't be about religion," Finn said. "Rachel was an atheist, while Laura and Sophie were devout."

Sheila nodded. "And they come from different backgrounds. Laura was a teacher, Sophie a volunteer, and Rachel a high-powered executive. Different education levels, different income brackets."

"The only common thread is that they're all women in their twenties," Finn said, his brow furrowed in concentration.

Sheila sighed, running a hand through her hair. "There has to be something we're missing. Some connection we haven't found yet. Let's dig into Rachels' background more—maybe we'll come across some kind of transgression similar to the infidelity Laura and Sophie were involved with."

"I'll start with her social media," Finn said, opening his laptop. "You take her financials?"

Sheila nodded, pulling up Rachel's bank statements on her own computer. The room fell silent save for the soft tapping of keyboards and occasional mouse clicks.

Sheila's fingers flew over the keyboard, eyes scanning the rows of transactions in Rachel's bank statements. She noted regular expenses: groceries, utility bills, and a hefty mortgage payment. Everything seemed typical for someone of Rachel's wealth. High-end restaurant charges, frequent spa visits, and donations to various charities were all present but expected. There were no suspicious withdrawals or unexplained expenses.

Sheila sighed, frustration mounting. "Nothing unusual here," she murmured to herself. She moved on to Rachel's investments and savings accounts, finding them in order and consistent with her affluent lifestyle. She glanced over at Finn, who was still engrossed in Rachel's social media.

"Any luck on your end?" she asked, hoping for a breakthrough.

Finn shook his head. "Not unless you count posting too many videos of her Shih Tzu as a sin. You?"

Sheila shook her head, gesturing at her screen full of spreadsheets. "Her finances are immaculate. No unexpected withdrawals, no suspicious transfers. She didn't even miss a credit card payment. As far as I can tell, she was a model citizen. No affairs, no financial irregularities, not even a parking ticket."

Finn leaned back in his chair, stretching. "Maybe we're looking at this all wrong. What if the killer just knows all the victims personally? Could be killing them for reasons we don't understand yet."

Sheila considered this. It wasn't an angle they had explored thoroughly. "Okay, let's run with that. We need to cross-reference their social circles, see if there's any overlap we missed."

Finn nodded, cracking his knuckles before turning back to his computer. "I'll start with Laura Hastings. You take Sophie Tournay?"

"Got it," Sheila replied, pulling up Sophie's social media profiles.

They worked in focused silence, the only sounds the clicking of keyboards and occasional mouse scrolls. Sheila meticulously went through Sophie's friend lists on various platforms, jotting down names that appeared frequently or seemed significant.

"Anything?" Finn asked.

Sheila shook her head. "Nothing concrete. Sophie's circles seem to be mostly other volunteers and church members. You?"

"Similar story with Laura." Finn sighed. "Lots of teacher friends, some family. No obvious connections to Sophie or Rachel so far."

Sheila pressed on, expanding her search to include work colleagues, gym memberships, and even grocery store loyalty programs. Her eyes burned from staring at the screen, but she forced herself to focus.

"Wait," she said suddenly, sitting up straighter. "Laura and Sophie both attended a charity gala four years ago. Different tables, but same event. It was called 'Coldwater Cares: A Night of Hope and Healing.'"

Finn leaned over to look at her screen. "Good catch. What was the event about?"

Sheila quickly scanned the event description. "It was a fundraiser for local mental health initiatives. Looks like it drew quite a crowd from different sectors of the community."

"Any sign of Rachel there?" Finn asked.

Sheila scrolled through the event photos. "No, it doesn't look like it." She swallowed hard, disappointed.

"Hold on, I think I have something," Finn said. He turned his laptop toward Sheila, pointing at a social media post from the event. It was a group photo. In the background, barely visible, were Laura Hastings and Sophie Tournay.

"What am I looking at?" Sheila asked, puzzled. "I already told you they both attended the event."

"See this guy?" Finn asked, pointing to a tall, broad-shouldered man with dark hair slicked back and a neatly trimmed beard standing off to the side.

His fingers flew over the keyboard as he pulled up another photo, this one from a corporate event at Elbridge Tech. There, shaking hands with Rachel Kim, was the same man from the charity event photo.

"Who is that?" Sheila asked, her pulse quickening.

Finn zoomed in on the man's name tag. "Juan Rodriguez. Let's look him up." He tapped away at his keyboard. "Apparently he's a local businessman, owns a chain of health food stores in the area."

Sheila's mind raced. "How did we miss this connection before?"

"He's not prominently featured in any of these photos," Finn said. "Just in the background or periphery. Easy to overlook if you're not specifically looking for him."

Sheila went back to her own computer to research this new suspect. "Rodriguez is forty-five years old, born and raised in Coldwater," she said. "According to this, he started his health food store chain, 'Nature's Way,' about fifteen years ago. It's grown to six locations across the county."

Finn nodded, taking notes. "Any priors?"

Sheila shook her head. "Clean record. But look at this," she said, pointing to her screen. "Rodriguez's stores specialize in herbal remedies and supplements. Including, get this, ipecac syrup."

Finn's eyebrows shot up. "The same substance used to poison Jason Reeves?"

Sheila nodded grimly. "Exactly. Doesn't explain how he could've poisoned Jason, but it's clear he'd have no trouble getting his hands on the poison. And there's more. Rodriguez is deeply involved in his local church, St. Michael's. He even runs a men's group that focuses on 'maintaining moral purity in a corrupt world.'"

"That could explain the religious angle," Finn said. "But what about Rachel? She was an atheist."

"Maybe she rejected his advances?" Sheila suggested. "Or maybe she knew something about him, something he couldn't risk getting out. There could be all kinds of reasons we haven't figured out."

She paused, thinking. "We really just need to talk to him. Maybe—"

"Hold on," Finn murmured. "I've got a news article here. Apparently, last year, Rodriguez tried to get the school board to implement a 'purity pledge' for high school students. It didn't pass, but guess who was one of the most vocal opponents?"

"Rachel Kim?" Sheila asked.

"Exactly. She gave a speech at the board meeting, calling the pledge 'regressive and harmful.'"

They looked at each other as the implications of their discovery set in. Juan Rodriguez had connections to all three victims, access to the poison used on Jason Reeves, and a history of extreme views on morality and purity.

"Let's go find this guy," Sheila said, rising.

CHAPTER SIXTEEN

Sheila's fingers drummed impatiently on the steering wheel as she and Finn made their way to Juan Rodriguez's home. The afternoon traffic in Coldwater was light, but every red light felt like an eternity.

"What's our approach here?" Finn asked, reviewing their notes on his tablet.

Sheila took a deep breath, considering. "We keep it casual at first. We're just following up on a lead, asking some routine questions. No need to spook him if he's innocent."

"And if he's not?"

"Then we'll be ready," Sheila replied, her hand unconsciously moving to check her holstered weapon.

They pulled up to a modest two-story house in a quiet suburban neighborhood. Colorful flowerbeds lined the walkway, and a 'Nature's Way' bumper sticker adorned the SUV in the driveway.

They approached the front door, and Sheila rang the bell. No answer. She tried again, then knocked firmly. Still nothing.

"Car's here," she muttered. "He should be home."

Just as they were about to leave, the door opened slightly, held by a security chain. A man's face appeared in the gap: Juan Rodriguez, looking exactly like his photos, but with an expression of wariness that hadn't been captured on camera.

"Can I help you?" he asked, his voice guarded.

Sheila held up her badge. "Mr. Rodriguez? I'm Deputy Stone, and this is Deputy Mercer. We'd like to ask you a few questions if you have a moment."

Rodriguez's eyes widened slightly. "What's this about?"

"Just following up on a lead, sir," Finn said smoothly. "Nothing to worry about. May we come in?"

Rodriguez hesitated, then nodded reluctantly. He closed the door, and they heard the chain being removed before he opened it fully. "Come in," he said, gesturing them inside.

The interior of the house was immaculate, with a distinctly minimalist aesthetic. Rodriguez led them to a living room dominated by a large cross on one wall and shelves filled with health and spirituality books.

"Please, sit," he said, indicating the couch. He remained standing, his posture tense. "Now, what's this all about?"

Sheila decided to start gently. "Mr. Rodriguez, we understand you attended the 'Coldwater Cares' charity gala four years ago. Is that correct?"

He nodded slowly. "Yes, I try to attend most local charity events. My business does a lot of community outreach."

"Do you recall meeting Laura Hastings or Sophie Tournay at that event?" Finn asked.

Rodriguez's brow furrowed. "Those names sound familiar... Wait, aren't those the women who were murdered recently?"

Sheila noticed a slight tremor in his hand as he said this. Nervousness? Or guilt? "That's right," she said. "We're trying to establish any connections between the victims."

Rodriguez's face paled. "You...you don't think *I* had anything to do with those murders, do you?"

"We're just exploring all possibilities, Mr. Rodriguez," Finn said calmly. "Can you tell us about your relationship with these women?"

Rodriguez ran a hand through his hair, visibly agitated. "I...I didn't really know them. I mean, I might have met them at the gala, but I meet lots of people at those events."

"And Rachel Kim?" Sheila asked.

"I knew her from some school board meetings, but that's it."

Sheila leaned forward. "Mr. Rodriguez, we know that you run a men's group at St. Michael's Church focusing on moral purity. Can you tell us more about that?"

His eyes narrowed. "What does that have to do with anything? Are you implying something?"

"We're not implying anything," Sheila said, keeping her voice level. "We're just trying to understand the full picture."

Rodriguez stood abruptly. "I think I'd like you to leave now. If you have any more questions, you can contact my lawyer."

Sheila and Finn exchanged a glance. This wasn't going well. "Mr. Rodriguez," Sheila began, "we're not here to accuse you of anything. We're just—"

"I know my rights," Rodriguez interrupted. "And I know what you're insinuating. I'm a respected businessman and a valuable member of this community. I had nothing to do with those murders."

The tension in the room was palpable. Rodriguez stood with his arms crossed, his face a mask of indignation and fear. Sheila remained seated, trying to project calm while internally strategizing her next move.

"Mr. Rodriguez," she began, keeping her voice even, "I understand this is upsetting, but we have a job to do. These women were murdered, and we need to follow every lead."

Rodriguez's jaw clenched. "And I'm telling you, I'm not a lead. I'm a victim here—a victim of your baseless suspicions!"

Finn leaned forward. "Sir, if you're innocent, then helping us will only clear your name faster."

"I shouldn't have to prove my innocence!" Rodriguez snapped.

Suddenly, a memory clicked into place in Sheila's mind—Francine Albright, the elderly woman from St. Michael's. She had mentioned seeing a 'new priest' at the church recently.

Sheila's pulse quickened. If they could get Rodriguez in a lineup, Francine could potentially identify whether he was the man she saw. It wasn't conclusive evidence, but it could be a significant step forward—or it might completely exonerate Rodriguez.

"Mr. Rodriguez," Sheila said, her tone shifting to something more conciliatory, "I have a proposition for you. One that could clear this up quickly."

Rodriguez eyed her warily. "What kind of proposition?"

"We have a witness who saw a man at St. Michael's recently—a man she didn't recognize, who was presenting himself as a priest. If you'd be willing to participate in a lineup, we could potentially rule you out as a suspect immediately."

Rodriguez's expression wavered between suspicion and hope. "A lineup? But I haven't done anything wrong."

"Exactly," Finn said, catching on to Sheila's plan. "If our witness doesn't identify you, that's a major point in your favor. It could end our inquiries into your involvement right here and now."

Rodriguez seemed to consider this, his anger slowly giving way to calculation. "And if I refuse?"

Sheila chose her words carefully. "That's your right. But it would leave us with unanswered questions. We'd have to continue our investigation, which might involve speaking to your employees, your church group members..."

She let the implication hang in the air. Rodriguez's reputation was clearly important to him, and the mere suggestion of a prolonged public investigation seemed to unsettle him.

After a long moment, Rodriguez sighed heavily. "Fine. I'll do your lineup. But I want it on record that I'm cooperating under protest, and I reserve the right to have my lawyer present."

Sheila nodded, relief washing over her. "Of course. We appreciate your cooperation, Mr. Rodriguez. If you'd be willing to come down to the station now, we can get this taken care of quickly."

As they led Rodriguez out to their car, Sheila caught Finn's eye. They both knew this was a gamble. If Francine identified Rodriguez, it would strengthen their case against him. But if she didn't...

They'd be back to square one, with a killer still on the loose and time running out.

***

Sheila stood behind the one-way glass, watching as Francine Albright squinted at the lineup. Juan Rodriguez stood among five other men of similar build and age, all dressed identically. Ms. Albright had been studying them for what felt like an eternity.

"Take your time, Ms. Albright," Sheila said into the intercom, trying to keep the impatience out of her voice. "There's no rush."

Francine nodded, her eyes moving from one man to the next. "I...I'm not sure," she said, her voice wavering. "It was weeks ago, you know. My memory isn't what it used to be."

Sheila exchanged a glance with Finn. This wasn't going as smoothly as they'd hoped.

"It's okay, Ms. Albright," Sheila said, stepping into the room. "Let's talk through it. What do you remember about the man you saw at the church?"

Francine's brow furrowed in concentration. "He was tall...well-dressed. He had kind eyes, I remember that."

Sheila nodded encouragingly. "That's good. Anything else? Maybe something unique about his appearance?"

Francine shook her head, frustration evident on her face. "I'm sorry, I just can't be certain. They all look similar from here."

Sheila felt her heart sink. Without a positive identification, they had nothing concrete to tie Rodriguez to the crimes—or to exonerate him. She took a deep breath, reminding herself to remain patient.

"It's alright, Ms. Albright. Let's try something else. Close your eyes for a moment."

Francine did as instructed.

"Now, think back to that day at the church. You're standing there, and this man approaches you. What's the first thing you notice about him?"

Francine's eyes remained closed, her face scrunched in concentration. "His smile," she said slowly. "He had a warm smile. And...and there was something about his face..."

Sheila leaned in, sensing they were on the verge of a breakthrough. "What about his face, Ms. Albright?"

"It was…strange, like he was wearing a lot of makeup. Odd for a priest."

Finn scribbled in his notebook, taking down these details.

"Do you notice anything else about him?" Sheila asked.

Suddenly, Francine's eyes snapped open. "Oh! I remember now! He had a small scar, just above his right eyebrow. It was faint, but I noticed it when he got close."

Sheila's heart raced as she turned to look at the lineup. Juan Rodriguez's face was unblemished.

"Are you sure about the scar, Ms. Albright?" she asked.

Francine nodded emphatically. "Yes, yes, I'm certain now. None of these men have that scar. The man I saw at the church isn't here."

Sheila's heart sank—they hadn't found their killer. Still, at least they had eliminated a suspect. It was progress, even if it meant they were back to square one.

Just then, Finn's phone rang. He stepped aside to answer it, his expression growing serious as he listened. When he hung up, he turned to Sheila with a grim look.

"We've got a situation," he said quietly as he led Sheila out of Francine's hearing. "Someone left a message in the town square…and the chief thinks it's from the Coldwater Confessor."

CHAPTER SEVENTEEN

Sheila and Finn arrived at Coldwater's central plaza as the late afternoon sun cast long shadows across the brick-paved square. A crowd had gathered around the statue of the town's founder, where a pristine white envelope had been taped to the bronze plaque. The air was thick with tension and the murmur of speculation from onlookers.

Crime scene technicians were already at work, carefully removing the envelope and placing it in an evidence bag. Sheila approached, her heart racing, acutely aware of the eyes of both her colleagues and the public upon her.

"What have we got?" she asked the lead technician, trying to keep her voice steady.

"Single page letter, handwritten," he replied, handing her the bagged document. "No fingerprints on initial examination, but we'll do a more thorough check back at the lab. The paper seems to be high-quality."

Sheila slipped on a pair of latex gloves and carefully extracted the letter. As she began to read, her brow furrowed in confusion. The handwriting was neat, almost calligraphic, adding an unsettling air of formality to the message.

"What is it?" Finn asked, peering over her shoulder.

"It's...some kind of religious manifesto," Sheila replied, her eyes scanning the page. "But it's not like anything I've seen before. The language is...archaic, almost Biblical in tone."

The letter was indeed a rambling discourse, filled with unfamiliar religious terminology and apocalyptic warnings. Sheila read aloud:

"Hearken, ye citizens of Coldwater, for the time of the Eternal Convergence is upon us, and the Celestial Hierarchy demands purity. I am but a humble servant of the Divine Paradigm tasked with cleansing the world of its transgressors. The tide is at its flood, the hour grows late. The sins of mankind cry out for judgment."

She skipped down a few lines:

"Each soul I send to judgment brings us closer to the Great Awakening. The sinful must be purged so that the righteous may ascend to the Empyrean Realm. Know that my work, though it may seem cruel to mortal eyes, is a mercy. For in death, the impure are given the chance for redemption that they squandered in life."

Finn shook his head. "What the hell is he talking about? It's like a mashup of a dozen different religions."

Sheila continued reading:

"To those who would stand in the way of the Divine Mission, know that your efforts are futile. The Cosmic Order cannot be denied, and the Cleansing will continue until the appointed hour. The stars themselves bear witness to my holy task, and the constellations guide my hand."

She looked up at Finn, her face grim. "It goes on like this for another page. References to obscure religious concepts, threats of more 'cleansing'. There's also mention of specific constellations: Orion, Cassiopeia, and Ursa Major. Could be significant. It's signed 'The Instrument of Divine Justice'."

Chief Dawson, who had arrived on the scene, joined them, looking worried. "Is this actually from our killer, or just some nutjob looking for attention?"

Sheila examined the letter closely. "There's a seal at the bottom—some kind of intricate symbol I've never seen before. It looks like it was stamped with a custom seal. What is that design? Thorns?"

"It's hard to imagine a copycat coming up with this level of originality," Finn said. "My guess is this is the real deal."

Sheila nodded. "I think so, too. He's revealing more of his ideology, like he wants us to understand his mission."

"But what does it mean?" Chief Dawson asked, frustration evident in his voice. "Is he giving us clues, or just spouting nonsense? And why go public now?"

Sheila read through the letter again. "He's positioning himself as some kind of divine judge, cleansing the world of sin. But these religious references...I've never heard of half of these terms. 'Eternal Convergence', 'Divine Paradigm', 'Empyrean Realm'...it's like he's created his own religion, or cobbled together pieces from various obscure beliefs."

"Or he's part of some cult we've never encountered," Finn suggested. "Maybe there are others who believe this stuff."

"That's a scary thought," Chief Dawson muttered. "One killer is bad enough. A group of them..."

Sheila ran a hand through her hair, thinking. "We need to research these terms, see if we can trace them to any known religious groups. And we need to analyze every word of this letter for potential clues about his next move. The mentions of specific constellations could be important—maybe they relate to timing or locations of his attacks."

"Maybe our killer has a background in astronomy," Finn said. "It would explain the star references and could narrow down our suspect pool."

"There's something else," Sheila said, pointing to a paragraph near the end of the letter. "He mentions 'seven seals' that need to be broken before the 'Great Cleansing' can be completed. Could he be planning seven murders?"

"God help us if that's true," Dawson murmured. "Four more murders." He ran a hand over his face. "The press is going to have a field day with this. We need to get ahead of it, maybe release a statement..."

"Not yet," Sheila said. "We need to control the information. If we release details, we might inspire copycats or cause a panic. Let's analyze the letter thoroughly first, see what we're dealing with."

"Okay," Dawson said hesitantly. "But don't drag your feet on this. If we don't speak to the press soon and control the narrative…there's no telling what conspiracy theories others might hatch."

***

"This doesn't make any sense," Sheila muttered, scrolling through yet another online forum about apocalyptic religions. "None of these terms—Eternal Convergence, Divine Paradigm, Empyrean Realm—show up anywhere in the mainstream or even fringe religious groups. It's like he made it all up."

She and Finn were back at the precinct, their faces illuminated by the glow of their computer screens. Books and printouts were strewn across the desk, each one related to obscure religious texts or astrological charts. The remnants of their last meal—takeout containers and half-empty coffee cups—cluttered the table, a testament to their relentless pursuit of answers. Sheila rubbed her temples, feeling the weight of exhaustion and frustration settling in.

Finn glanced over from his screen, where he was attempting to cross-reference the constellations mentioned in the manifesto. The soft click of his mouse and the rhythmic tapping of his keyboard punctuated the silence.

"Yeah, and the constellations don't lead us anywhere, either," he said. "I've looked into astrological interpretations, historical references, everything. There's nothing concrete that ties Orion, Cassiopeia, and Ursa Major together in any significant way."

Sheila sighed, leaning back in her chair. "So we have a killer who thinks he's on some divine mission, but we can't trace his beliefs or find a pattern to his actions."

The room felt stifling, the air thick with their combined frustration. The small clock on the wall ticked away the minutes, a constant reminder of the time slipping through their fingers.

Finn tried to offer a reassuring smile. "We'll figure it out, Sheila. We've cracked tougher cases than this before."

Sheila's eyes met his, but she felt distant, disconnected. "I don't know. This one feels different. He's meticulous, and every move is calculated. And this 'seven seals' business... What if he really *is* planning seven murders? What if we can't stop him?"

Finn reached out, placing a hand on her shoulder. His touch was warm, a stark contrast to the cold dread that had settled in her chest. "Hey, we'll stop him. We're good at this. We've got the team, the resources. We'll find the connection and put an end to this."

Sheila looked away, her mind racing with the thought of the seven seals. "But what if we don't? What if he targets another woman? We have no idea who his next victim might be or why he's chosen them. We can't protect everyone in Coldwater."

Finn squeezed her shoulder gently. "We can't think like that. We have to focus on the facts, follow the evidence. We'll figure out his pattern and catch him before he strikes again."

Sheila nodded absently, her thoughts spiraling. She glanced at the whiteboard on the wall, covered in photos of the victims and snippets of the manifesto. The smiling faces of Laura Hastings, Sophie Tournay, and Rachel Kim looked back at her, a haunting reminder of their failure to prevent their deaths.

"There's got to be something we're missing," she said, more to herself than to Finn. She leaned forward, tapping a pen against her notebook. "Maybe it's not about the constellations themselves, but what they represent. Orion, the hunter. Cassiopeia, the queen. Ursa Major, the great bear. They all have stories, myths attached to them."

Finn's brow furrowed in concentration. "So you think he's choosing these constellations for their symbolic meanings?"

"Maybe," Sheila replied. "Or maybe they're part of his twisted ritual. But why those three? What connects them?"

Finn stood up and began pacing the small office. "If we can figure out what those constellations mean to him, we might get closer to understanding his motives. But right now, it's like trying to put together a puzzle without all the pieces."

Sheila watched him pace, her mind working overtime. She felt the pressure mounting, the weight of the victims' families' grief pressing down on her. She thought about Chief Dawson's words earlier, the urgency in his voice. The media would be relentless when they caught wind of the manifesto. They needed answers, and they needed them fast.

The phone on the desk rang, jolting Sheila out of her thoughts. She picked it up, hoping for a lead, but it was just another reporter fishing for information. She hung up, her frustration boiling over.

"Every second we waste, he's getting closer to his next victim," Sheila said, her voice trembling with anger and fear. "We can't keep hitting dead ends. There has to be something we're overlooking."

She ran a hand through her hair, frustrated. She was usually the strong one, the pillar of determination, but this case was wearing her down. It felt like the killer was taunting them, dancing just out of reach.

Suddenly, Finn's phone buzzed with a notification. He glanced at it, his eyes widening. "Sheila, come look at this."

Sheila hurried over, peering at the screen. It was a message from one of their contacts in the tech department. They'd gotten a hit on the seal from the letter. Apparently it was a custom design, very rare, sold by a store in town called Sanctuary of the Celestial Path.

Sheila was already on her feet. "I think it's time we go pay them a visit," she said.

CHAPTER EIGHTEEN

"I know Coldwater pretty well, but I have to say this is one place I've never visited," Sheila said.

The sun was setting as she and Finn pulled up to the Sanctuary of the Celestial Path. The store was tucked away in a quiet corner of Coldwater's historic district, its weathered brick facade adorned with intricate celestial designs. A neon sign in the window flickered weakly, casting an eerie blue glow over the sidewalk.

"Not exactly your scene?" Finn asked as they exited the car.

"I'm a little more…scientifically-minded," Sheila said, her eyes scanning the storefront. The display window was filled with an eclectic mix of crystals, tarot cards, and astrological charts. A sense of unease settled in her stomach as they approached the entrance.

A bell chimed softly as they pushed open the heavy wooden door. The interior was scented with a heady mix of incense and herbs. Shelves lined the walls, packed with books, candles, and various mystical paraphernalia.

Behind the counter stood a woman in her fifties, her silver hair pulled back in a tight bun. She wore flowing robes covered in astrological symbols, and her neck was adorned with multiple crystal pendants.

"Welcome to the Sanctuary," she said, her voice low and melodious. "How may I assist you on your spiritual journey today?"

Sheila approached the counter, subtly flashing her badge. "Good evening. I'm Deputy Stone, and this is Deputy Mercer. We'd like to ask you a few questions about a product you sell here."

The woman's serene expression faltered for a moment before she regained her composure. "Of course, Deputies. I'm Celeste, the owner. What would you like to know?"

Finn produced a photo of the seal from the killer's letter. "We're interested in this custom seal. Our sources tell us it was purchased here."

Celeste's eyes widened as she looked at the photo. "Yes, I remember this design. It's quite unique. But I'm afraid I can't disclose information about our customers without a warrant."

Sheila leaned in, her voice low and urgent. "Celeste, this is part of an ongoing murder investigation. Any information you provide could save lives."

Celeste's eyes darted nervously around. "I...I'm sorry, but I really don't know anything about who bought that seal. We have many customers, and I can't remember them all."

Sheila was about to press further when she heard a muffled noise from the back of the store. Her eyes narrowed. "Is someone else here?"

Celeste's posture stiffened, her hands fidgeting with the crystals around her neck. "Oh, that's just…someone I hired for part-time help. To organize the stockroom."

There was no mistaking the hesitation in Celeste's voice. Sheila exchanged a quick glance with Finn, seeing her own suspicion mirrored in his eyes.

"Mind if we talk to this helper?" Sheila asked, her tone making it clear it wasn't really a question.

"I...I don't think that's necessary," Celeste stammered. "He's very shy, you see, and—"

Sheila cut her off. "Celeste, I get the feeling you're not being entirely truthful with us. Who's really back there?"

Before Celeste could answer, the beaded curtain separating the main shop from the back room parted. A young man stepped out, freezing when he saw the deputies.

For a moment, time seemed to stand still. Then Celeste's voice shattered the silence.

"Run, Jasper!" she shouted.

The young man's eyes widened in panic. Without hesitation, he turned and bolted for the door.

"Stop! Police!" Sheila yelled, already in pursuit. As she raced after the fleeing suspect, Sheila could hear Finn behind her, calling for backup.

Sheila rushed through a dark room, then shouldered open a door swinging shut behind the fleeing Jasper. She burst out onto the street, nearly colliding with a group of tourists.

"Stop!" she yelled as the suspect darted down an alley.

She followed Jasper through a maze of narrow passages between old buildings. Her heart pounded as she vaulted over a stack of crates, her eyes never leaving the fleeing figure ahead.

Jasper emerged onto a busy street, weaving through startled pedestrians. Sheila followed, her lungs burning as she pushed herself to keep up. She could no longer hear Finn behind her. Had he fallen behind or taken a different route?

As they approached a construction site, Jasper scaled a chain-link fence with surprising agility. Sheila gritted her teeth and followed, ignoring the bite of metal on her palms.

The chase continued through the half-built structure, a dangerous obstacle course of exposed beams and scattered tools. Sheila's foot caught on a coil of wire, sending her stumbling. She recovered quickly, but the momentary delay allowed Jasper to increase his lead.

Emerging from the construction site, she found herself in a small park. Jasper headed for a dense copse of trees, clearly hoping to lose his pursuers in the gathering darkness.

Sheila pushed herself harder, closing the gap. Just as Jasper reached the treeline, she made a desperate lunge, tackling him to the ground.

They rolled across the damp grass, grappling for control. Despite his initial panic, Jasper fought with unexpected strength. Sheila managed to pin him down, her voice harsh as she gasped for breath.

"Stop resisting! You're under arrest!"

Finn arrived moments later, quickly cuffing the still-struggling suspect. As they hauled him to his feet, Sheila got her first good look at his face. He was younger than she'd expected, probably in his early twenties, with wide, frightened eyes.

"Why'd you run?" she demanded.

"I'll never talk to you," he said, his face hardening. "You can't stop what's already been set in motion."

***

Sheila stood in the observation room, her eyes flicking between the two monitors showing the separate interrogation rooms. In one, Jasper sat rigid and defiant, his jaw clenched. In the other, Celeste seemed to have aged a decade since their encounter at the shop, her earlier mystical demeanor replaced by a look of weary resignation.

Sheila's stomach churned with a mix of anticipation and dread. These two might hold the key to unraveling the mystery of the Coldwater Confessor, but extracting that information wouldn't be easy. She took a deep breath, centering herself. Years of experience had taught her that interrogations were as much about patience and psychology as they were about asking the right questions.

"What do you think?" Finn asked. "You take one, I'll take the other?"

After a moment's consideration, Sheila decided to start with Jasper. His youth and bravado might make him more likely to slip up.

"I'll take Jasper," she said. "Afterward we can compare notes."

"Sounds like a deal," Finn said as he left the room.

Sheila took another deep breath, steeling herself before entering Jasper's interrogation room. The young man glared at her as she sat down across from him. "I told you, I'm not talking," he said, his voice laced with defiance.

Sheila leaned back, projecting an air of calm. "That's fine, Jasper. I'll do the talking for now." She opened a file folder, making a show of reviewing its contents. The rustling of papers filled the tense silence. "You've got quite an interesting background. Dropped out of college two years ago, started working at your aunt's shop. But before that, you were studying astrophysics. Quite a change."

A flicker of surprise crossed Jasper's face before he masked it. Sheila noticed the slight widening of his eyes, the momentary tension in his shoulders. She pressed on, her voice casual but probing.

"What made you give up on the stars, Jasper? Or did you just find a different way to pursue them?"

Jasper's eyes narrowed, but he remained silent. His fingers drummed a nervous rhythm on the table.

Sheila changed tactics, her tone softening. "You know, your aunt is in the other room right now. She seemed pretty upset. I wonder what she's telling my partner."

Jasper's composure cracked slightly. A muscle twitched in his jaw. "Aunt Celeste wouldn't say anything. She believes in the cause."

"The cause?" Sheila asked, leaning forward slightly. "You mean the 'Divine Paradigm'? The 'Eternal Convergence'? Tell me, Jasper, do you really believe in all that?"

For the first time, uncertainty flickered in Jasper's eyes. He shifted in his seat, his gaze dropping to the table. "You...you wouldn't understand. It's bigger than you can imagine."

"Then help me understand, Jasper. People are dying. If this cause is so important, so meaningful, make me see it."

For a moment, it seemed like Jasper might break. His lips parted, a conflicted look crossing his face. But then the shutters came down again. He crossed his arms and leaned back, his expression hardening. "I've got nothing more to say."

Sheila leaned forward, her voice softening. "Jasper, I know you believe in this cause. But people are dying. Innocent people. Is that really what you want?"

Jasper's eyes flickered, a hint of doubt crossing his face before it hardened again. "You don't understand. Sometimes sacrifices are necessary for the greater good."

"Greater good?" Sheila asked. "What greater good could possibly justify murder? Help me understand, Jasper. If your cause is so important, make me see it."

Jasper remained silent, his jaw clenched.

Sheila changed tactics. "Look, I get it. You're protecting someone. But think about this: If you cooperate, tell us what you know, we can work something out—reduced charges, maybe even immunity."

For a moment, Jasper seemed to consider this. His fingers twitched on the table. But then he shook his head. "I'm not a snitch."

Frustration building, Sheila tried one last approach. "Let's talk about the stars, Jasper. You studied astrophysics, right? What drew you to that field?"

For the first time, a spark of interest lit Jasper's eyes. "The vastness of it all," he said softly. "The patterns, the cosmic dance of celestial bodies..."

"And how does that relate to this new belief system of yours?" Sheila asked.

Jasper's expression closed off again. "Nice try," he muttered. "But I'm done talking."

Realizing this was going nowhere, Sheila stood up, her chair scraping against the floor. "Think about what I said, Jasper. This is your chance to do the right thing."

She left the room, the door closing behind her with a soft click. In the hallway, she leaned against the wall, closing her eyes for a moment. Jasper's unwavering belief in this 'cause' was troubling. It spoke to a level of indoctrination that wouldn't be easily broken.

Could the killer have a group of adherents, all of them subscribing to the same deluded beliefs the killer used to justify murder? The very possibility caused Sheila to shudder.

The door to Celeste's interrogation room opened, and Finn stepped out, looking clear-eyed and thoughtful.

"Well, I've softened her up for you," he said. "I think all she needs now is a woman's touch. Should I talk to the kid?"

Sheila shook her head. "Give him some time."

As she entered Celeste's interrogation room, she noticed the older woman's hands trembling slightly. Celeste's eyes were red-rimmed, her earlier composure completely shattered.

"Mrs. Moon," Sheila began gently, taking a seat across from her. "We're not here to cause trouble for you or your nephew. We just want to understand what's going on. People have died, and we need to prevent more deaths. Can you help us with that?"

Celeste's eyes welled with tears. "I...I never wanted anyone to get hurt," she whispered, her voice cracking. "It wasn't supposed to be like this."

Sheila leaned forward, sensing a breakthrough. She kept her voice soft, sympathetic. "Tell me about the man who came to your shop, Celeste. The one who bought the custom seal."

Celeste hesitated, glancing toward the door as if expecting Jasper to burst in and stop her. Her fingers twisted the hem of her flowing shirt, now wrinkled and stained with tears. Finally, she began to speak, her words coming out in a rush.

"He came to the shop about six months ago, talking about the stars and divine judgment. At first, I thought he was just another New Age enthusiast. We get a lot of those, you know. But there was something...compelling about him. He spoke with such conviction, such certainty. It was like he could see things the rest of us couldn't."

"What did he look like?" Sheila asked, her pen poised over her notepad.

Celeste's brow furrowed in concentration. "He was...average. Medium height, medium build. Long, shaggy brown hair."

"Did he have a small scar just above his right eyebrow, by any chance?" Sheila asked, recalling Francine Albright's description.

Celeste frowned. "I don't think so."

"Did he look like he was wearing makeup?"

"Not that I recall."

Sheila took a long breath, calming herself. By the sound of it, this was not the same man Francine Albright had seen. Francine had described the priest as having hair that was gray and 'very neat,' not long, shaggy, and brown.

"He talked about the stars a lot," Celeste continued. "Said they held the key to understanding God's plan. Jasper was fascinated. I think...I think that's why he dropped out of school. To devote himself to this new...philosophy, I guess you'd call it."

"And what about you? Did you buy into this philosophy, too?"

Celeste licked her lips. "I…it seemed harmless enough, you know? And for the first time ever, it seemed like Jasper had a direction, a plan."

"Mrs. Moon, there's a good chance that the person you and your son spoke with was the Coldwater Confessor."

Celeste went pale. "I had no idea he was going to kill anyone," she said. "I thought it was all symbolic, spiritual—otherwise I never would've sold that seal to him."

"I know this may be difficult to answer, but it's important that you're completely truthful with me, for your son's sake as well as yours. Is it possible this man could've recruited Jasper?"

Celeste stared at Sheila in stunned silence for several seconds. "Are you asking whether Jasper could've had anything to do with the murders?"

Sheila waited, saying nothing.

"Absolutely not!" Celeste said. "Jasper may have gotten caught up in some strange ideas, but he's not a violent person. He wouldn't hurt anyone, no matter what philosophy he believes in."

Sheila nodded, her expression neutral. "I appreciate your conviction, Mrs. Moon. Can you tell me where you and Jasper were this morning?"

"We were at the shop, of course," Celeste replied, her voice steadier now. "We're always there during business hours. You can check the camera footage if you don't believe me."

Sheila raised an eyebrow. "You have camera footage?"

Celeste nodded. "Yes, we installed security cameras last year. I can access the feed on my phone if you'd like to see it."

"That would be helpful," Sheila said. "Let me get your phone for you."

A few minutes later, Celeste was swiping through the footage on her phone. Sheila watched intently, her eyes scanning for any sign of suspicious activity. The footage showed Celeste and Jasper going about their day, arranging displays and helping the occasional customer.

"Wait," Sheila said suddenly. "How far back does this footage go?"

"Not six months, if that's what you're looking for. It erases anything more than a month old."

Sheila's heart sank. So much for getting a look at the killer.

"What was your conversation like with the man who bought the seal?" she asked.

Celeste shrugged. "It was brief. He came in, asked about custom seals, and placed his order. He didn't engage in much small talk."

"Did he give a name?"

"John Smith," Celeste said with a wry smile. "Obviously fake, but it's not uncommon in our line of work. People value their privacy when it comes to spiritual matters."

"And he paid in cash?"

Celeste nodded. "Yes, that's also quite common."

"Have you heard from him since?" Sheila asked.

"No, not at all. He picked up the seal a week later, and that was the last I saw of him."

Sheila paused, considering her next question carefully. "Mrs. Moon, is there any possibility that Jasper has been in contact with this man without your knowledge?"

Celeste's eyes widened. "No, absolutely not. Jasper and I are very close. We work together every day, and he lives in the apartment above the shop. If he was meeting with someone or communicating regularly, I would know."

There was still one thing, however, that bothered Sheila. "If you and Jasper had nothing to do with the murders," she said, "then why did you tell Jasper to run?"

Celeste swallowed hard. "When you two came into the store and started asking questions, I figured this probably had to do with the Coldwater Confessor case. And since you were asking about the man who bought that seal…well, I guess I worried Jasper may have said or done something that would put him under suspicion—even a careless social media post these days can be damning."

"Why would Jasper post something potentially damning?"

Celeste sighed. "He means well, and he would never harm anyone…but not everyone knows that. Ever since the Patriot Act, there's no telling what might get you in trouble. He's dabbled in Communism, written posts about depopulating the earth...I guess I just thought there might be something worse that I didn't know about. I panicked."

Sheila studied the other woman in silence as she took this in.

"Please, Deputy Stone," Celeste said. "If anyone's in the wrong, it's me. I shouldn't have told him to run. Don't blame him for crimes he had nothing to do with."

Sheila nodded slowly and rose. "Thank you for your time, Mrs. Moon. We may have more questions later, but for now, I think we're done here."

Finn was waiting for her out in the hallway. "How'd it go?" he asked.

She sighed. "I was able to establish an alibi for the both of them this morning. Not sure whether that's good or bad news. Also, we need to look into Jasper's background—any suspicious social media posts, anything that might indicate motive for the murders."

"Already taken care of."

Sheila frowned, surprised. "What are you talking about?"

"Got him to show me those posts himself—tactless, yes, but not proof of anything. He didn't know any of the victims, didn't post anything about them specifically. Everything was vague, generic—wannabe bullshit."

"How'd you get him to reveal that to you?"

He shrugged. "Told him his silence would do his aunt a lot of harm. Leaned into that angle pretty hard, and he eventually caved."

"Well done," Sheila said.

Finn stretched his arms. "Were you able to get a description of the man who bought the seal?"

"Sort of. She said he had long, shaggy brown hair."

"That doesn't sound like the priest Francine met. Think one of them misremembered?"

"Maybe," Sheila murmured. "Or maybe they're both right."

"How could a man have long hair *and* short hair, unless—" He stopped, then smiled. "Huh. You think he wears a disguise? That would explain why Francine said he was wearing a lot of makeup."

Sheila nodded, her excitement growing the more she pondered this potential new lead. "And if he is wearing disguises, then he's got to get his materials somewhere."

"Sounds like it's time for you and me to check out some costume stores."

CHAPTER NINETEEN

The Father parked his car a few houses down from Emily Davis's modest two-story home. The quiet neighborhood was bathed in the soft glow of streetlights, but he saw no sign of Emily.

Yet.

He checked his watch: 9:17 PM. Surely she was still up. Her car was parked out front, so where was she? Taking a shower? He didn't want to approach the house until he was certain she was inside.

His heart rate quickened—not with nerves, but with anticipation. This was always the most exhilarating part: the moment before the hunt truly began.

He took a deep breath, centering himself. This wasn't about personal gratification. It was about fulfilling his divine mission.

As he breathed, his mind drifted to the letter he'd left in the town square. A smile played on his lips as he imagined the confusion it must be causing the police. The mixture of religious doctrines, the invented terms, the cosmic references: all carefully crafted to mislead and distract. Let them waste their time trying to decipher nonexistent clues while he continued his holy work.

Next, he thought about his earlier success with Jason Reeves. He chuckled softly, remembering how simple it had been to slip into the Spice Haven kitchen posing as a health inspector. While the panicked staff scrambled to address his fabricated concerns, he'd easily accessed the order meant for Reeves and laced it with ipecac syrup.

Child's play.

The sight of movement distracted him. Emily was pouring herself a cup of tea in the kitchen, her red hair catching the light as she stirred in some honey. Her phone lay on the counter, and she stared at it as if it contained the answers to life.

Such a small, mundane detail, but it spoke volumes about her character.

Frivolous. Focused on earthly conveniences rather than spiritual truth.

He reached into the glove compartment and pulled out the clerical collar. As he fastened it around his neck, he felt the familiar sense of righteousness wash over him. He wasn't just a man anymore. He was an instrument of divine will.

Next he reached into his bag, feeling the familiar cold weight of the candlestick. He had chosen it with care—cylindrical, heavy, and perfect for his holy work. He wasn’t just a man anymore. He was an instrument of divine will.

He slipped the candlestick into his voluminous coat pocket, then approached the front door and knocked. Emily opened the door slightly, her green eyes widening in recognition as she saw the clerical collar.

"Father? Can I help you?"

The Father smiled gently. "I’m terribly sorry to disturb you at this hour, child, but I was hoping you could spare a moment to discuss matters of the soul."

She hesitated, glancing behind her. "Um, now’s not really a good time..."

She's been following the news, he thought.

He stepped closer, his hand slipping into his coat pocket, fingers gripping the candlestick. "It’s never too late to find salvation. I can show you the way to something better than you've ever known—a way of peace and joy beyond anything you've ever experienced before."

Despite this good-natured invitation, Emily's worry seemed only to deepen. She swallowed hard, and a vein began to thrum in her neck. It was clear to the Father that she had no interest in accepting his offer.

Just as Emily tried to slam the door shut, the Father thrust his shoe in the gap, stopping it from closing. He shoved the door inward and made a grab for Emily, but she retreated, letting out a scream.

The Father pulled out the candlestick. "Don't say I didn't try to help," he said as he advanced into the room.

CHAPTER TWENTY

Sheila drummed her fingers on the steering wheel as she pulled into the parking lot of Spotlight Costumes.

I hope this isn't just a grand waste of time, she thought.

The realization that the killer might be using disguises had hit her like a lightning bolt. If she was right, it explained the discrepancies in witness descriptions and potentially widened their suspect pool significantly.

"You sure anyone's even here?" Finn asked from the passenger seat, stifling a yawn. "It's almost nine-thirty." They'd both been running on coffee and determination for the better part of the past forty-eight hours.

Sheila shrugged. "There's a light on."

"Doesn't mean they're open. A place like this probably closes at five or six."

"Well, they'll just have to make an exception for us. If our guy is using disguises, he has to get his supplies somewhere. Spotlight is the only professional costume shop in Coldwater. I'm not leaving without answers."

Finn chuckled softly.

"What?" Sheila asked, raising an eyebrow.

"You. Determined as always. Just don't give yourself an aneurysm, alright?"

Sheila rolled her eyes and got out of the vehicle.

As they approached the store's entrance, Sheila took in the colorful window display featuring everything from superhero costumes to Victorian-era gowns. The cheerful facade felt strangely at odds with their grim purpose.

Sheila tried the door—locked. A 'Closed' sign hung on the door.

"Well, that's a problem," Finn said dryly.

Sheila leaned closer, peering through the glass. Just then, she noticed a petite woman with graying hair in a bun striding by. Sheila rapped on the glass, and the woman jumped at the sound.

"I'm sorry, we're closed for the day!" the woman said.

Sheila held up her badge. "Deputy Stone, ma'am. This is Deputy Mercer. We need to speak with you."

The woman frowned, shaking her head. "I'm afraid I can't help you at this hour. Please come back during our regular business hours."

Finn leaned in, his voice low. "Maybe we should come back tomorrow, Sheila."

Sheila felt her frustration building. They needed this lead. "We're investigating a series of serious crimes. Your cooperation could be crucial."

The woman's resolve seemed to waver slightly, but she stood her ground. "I'm sorry, but I can't help you."

But Sheila wasn't ready to give up. "Ma'am, are you Sarah Jenkins, the owner?"

The woman nodded reluctantly.

"Mrs. Jenkins, I wouldn't be here this late if it wasn't absolutely necessary. Lives could be at stake. Please, just a few minutes of your time."

Sarah studied them for a long moment, conflict clear on her face. Finally, she sighed heavily. "Five minutes. Not a second more."

As Sarah unlocked the door, Sheila felt a mix of relief and anticipation. They were in, but the clock was ticking. They needed to make these five minutes count.

As they entered, Sheila was immediately struck by the organized chaos of the interior. Racks of costumes lined the walls, while shelves overflowed with wigs, masks, and makeup kits. The air smelled faintly of fabric and face paint.

"We can talk in my office," Sarah said, leading them to a small room in the back of the store. As they settled into chairs, Sheila noticed the walls were covered in photographs of elaborate costumes and stage makeup. It was clear Sarah took pride in her work.

"Mrs. Jenkins," Sheila began, "we're investigating a series of crimes that may involve the use of disguises. Have you had any customers recently who've made unusual or large purchases of prosthetics, wigs, or professional-grade makeup?"

Sarah's brow furrowed in concentration. "We get all sorts of requests here, especially around Halloween or when the Masquerade is putting on a show. But now that you mention it..." She trailed off, her eyes unfocusing as if trying to recall a distant memory.

"Yes?" Sheila asked, leaning forward slightly.

"There was a man," Sarah said slowly. "He's been in several times over the past year. Always very polite, but intense, you know? Said he was working on an independent film project."

Sheila felt a surge of excitement. This could be the lead they needed. "Can you describe him?"

Sarah shrugged. "Average height and build, I suppose. Brown hair. Nothing really stood out about him physically. But his eyes...they were striking. Very intense, almost...I don't know, haunted?"

"Do you have security cameras in the store?" Finn asked.

Sarah nodded. "Yes, we installed them last year after a series of shoplifting incidents. I can get you the footage if you'd like." Her earlier hesitation seemed to have completely evaporated, perhaps due to her excitement to help them crack this case. Sheila hoped that meant that her insistence on only giving them five minutes would be forgotten, as well.

While Finn went with Sarah to retrieve the security tapes, Sheila continued to look around the office, her mind humming with possibilities. If the killer was indeed using this shop for his disguises, they might finally have a solid lead.

Sarah returned with a laptop, setting it on the desk. "Here we go," she said, pulling up the security footage. "I've queued it to the last time I remember seeing him."

Sheila and Finn leaned in, their eyes fixed on the grainy black-and-white footage. They watched as a man entered the shop, his movements purposeful but unhurried. He spent time browsing the wig section before moving to the makeup counter.

The man's face was partially obscured by the angle of the camera, but Sheila could make out enough to see that he was indeed of average height and build, with brown hair. Francine had described him as having gray hair, but that may have been a wig.

Or, for that matter, the brown hair could be the wig. There was no telling.

"We'll need a copy of this footage," Sheila said, leaning back.

"Of course," Sarah said. "I'll copy the file onto a thumb drive."

Sheila tried to hold back her discouragement, but it was difficult. She'd hoped for something more concrete to go on, but thus far the footage had been of little use.

While Sarah copied the file, Sheila's eyes wandered across the room. Her gaze landed on a framed poster on the wall for a production of 'The Crucible' by the Masquerade theater group, starring several names she'd never heard of: Mike Goodell, Ezra Thorne, Elsa Maye. There was a second post from the same group for a production of Shakespeare's Julius Caesar.

A thought stirred in the back of Sheila's mind. She pulled out her phone, navigating to the picture she'd taken of the killer's letter.

"What is it?" Finn asked, stepping closer.

"Something he said in the letter," she murmured. She scanned the text. Most of it struck her as pseudo-religious jargon. But then her gaze fell on a particular phrase.

"The tide is at its flood," she said. "I could swear I've heard that before."

"Hamlet," Sarah said.

Sheila and Finn both turned to look at her.

"The actual quote," Sarah said, "goes, 'there is a tide in the affairs of men, which, taken at the flood, leads on to fortune; omitted, all the voyage of their life is bound in shallows and in miseries.'" She shrugged. "I did a lot of theater as a teenager."

"What about the Masquerade?" Sheila asked, pointing to the poster. "Do they do a lot of Shakespeare?"

Sarah nodded. "They did one of Hamlet just last year. I try to make it to as many of their shows as I can, not just because I love theater but also because they're our biggest clients. I've been providing costumes and makeup for their productions for years. In fact, their current director, Marcus Holloway, was just in last week discussing their upcoming show."

Sheila felt a chill run down her spine. The disguises, the theatrical supplies, the allusion to Shakespeare… Could it be that their killer wasn't just using disguises, but was actually involved in theater?

If so, it would explain his skill with disguises and his flair for the dramatic. But it also meant that there was no telling how much of his behavior was an act. The priest impersonation, the religious jargon in the letter—it might all be a ruse, a trick.

Which was to say, they might know even less about him than they'd thought.

Finn cleared his throat. "Where exactly does this group like to meet?"

***

Sheila guided the patrol car into the nearly empty parking lot of the Masquerade Theater. The imposing structure loomed before them, its Art Deco facade sticking out among the modern buildings surrounding it. Moonlight pooled on the cracked asphalt, giving the scene an eerie, almost abandoned feel.

A single vehicle, a sleek black Audi, sat in the parking lot.

"We should run those plates," Sheila told Finn as she cut the engine. The sudden silence was almost oppressive, broken only by the distant hum of traffic.

"And by 'we'," Finn said, "you mean 'me' right?"

"I was trying to be diplomatic, but yes."

While Finn called in the plates, Sheila studied the building. If the killer was involved in the world of theater, what were the chances he was involved in *this* theater? It was, as far as she knew, one of the only such places in the city—and certainly the largest—but still…

"Plates are registered to Marcus Holloway," Finn said a moment later. "The theater director."

Sheila nodded, a mixture of anticipation and apprehension coursing through her. "Let's go see if he's inside."

After checking to make sure the Audi was empty, Sheila and Finn approached the theater's grand entrance, its brass doors gleaming in the moonlight. Ornate carvings adorned the frame, telling stories of Greek myths and Shakespearean tragedies. Sheila tugged on the handle, surprised to find it unlocked.

"Hello?" she called out as they stepped into the cavernous lobby. Her voice echoed off the high ceilings and marble floors, seeming to multiply until it filled the space with a chorus of ghostly greetings.

The lobby was a testament to the theater's glory days, with ornate chandeliers, gilded mirrors, and plush red carpets. Faded posters of past productions lined the walls, silent witnesses to decades of performances. Sheila's eyes were drawn to a particularly striking poster for 'Phantom of the Opera,' the masked figure's eyes seeming to follow her as she moved.

"Mr. Holloway?" Finn called, his voice bouncing off the walls and returning to them unanswered.

They shared a look before proceeding deeper into the theater. Sheila's hand instinctively moved to her holstered weapon, a sense of unease growing with each step. The plush carpet muffled their footsteps, adding to the surreal atmosphere.

They passed through the main auditorium, rows of velvet seats stretching into the darkness like a sea of red waves. The air was thick with the musty scent of old fabric and wood polish. Sheila's flashlight beam cut through the gloom, dancing across the ornate moldings and faded murals on the ceiling.

The stage loomed before them, the heavy curtain half-drawn, revealing glimpses of an elaborate set. It appeared to be for a production of 'Macbeth,' with a foreboding castle facade and gnarled trees creating an ominous backdrop.

"Finn," Sheila whispered, her voice seeming too loud in the oppressive silence, "check the wings. I'll take the backstage area."

Finn nodded, moving off to the left while Sheila headed for the door marked 'Backstage.' She pushed it open slowly, wincing at the slight creak of the hinges.

Backstage was a maze of corridors and small rooms. Racks of costumes lined the walls, a riot of colors and textures in the beam of her flashlight. The air was thick with the scent of grease paint and sawdust, with an underlying mustiness that spoke of age and disuse.

Sheila's eyes darted from shadow to shadow, every nerve on high alert. She passed dressing rooms with stars on the doors, names long faded but still legible.

A sudden crash from somewhere ahead made Sheila freeze. Her heart pounded in her ears as she strained to listen. Another sound—footsteps, quick and light, moving away from her.

"Finn!" she called out, breaking into a run. "Someone's here!"

She rounded a corner and caught a glimpse of a figure darting across the far end of the corridor.

"Hey!" Sheila called out, increasing her speed. "Stop! Police!"

CHAPTER TWENTY ONE

Finn's head snapped up at the sound of Sheila's shout. "Stop! Police!" Her voice echoed through the cavernous theater, seeming to come from everywhere and nowhere at once.

"Sheila?" he called out, but only his own voice bounced back to him.

He started running, his footsteps muffled by the thick carpet of the lobby. The grand space quickly gave way to a labyrinth of narrow corridors backstage. Finn found himself in a maze of twisting passageways, each turn leading to more options. Props and costume racks lined the walls, creating strange shadows in the dim emergency lighting.

A life-sized mannequin loomed suddenly in front of him, its blank face startling in the gloom. Finn dodged around it, his heart pounding. The air was thick with the musty smell of old fabric and dust.

He paused at an intersection, straining his ears. Was that a footstep? A door closing? The building seemed to swallow sounds, making it impossible to pinpoint their origin.

"Sheila!" he called again, but there was no response.

Finn chose a corridor at random, picking up his pace. He passed dressing rooms, their doors ajar, mirrors reflecting slivers of the hallway and creating disorienting flashes of movement in his peripheral vision.

A crash from somewhere above made him skid to a stop. Finn looked up, trying to orient himself. The ceiling here was low, but he could see catwalks crisscrossing the space above the stage area.

Another sound—definitely footsteps this time—echoed from above. Finn's eyes darted around, searching for access to the upper levels. He spotted a metal ladder attached to the wall, partially hidden behind a rack of elaborate Victorian-era dresses.

Without hesitation, he began to climb. The metal was cold under his hands, and the ladder swayed slightly with his weight. As he neared the top, the sounds above grew louder. Whoever was up there wasn't trying to be quiet anymore.

Finn emerged onto a narrow catwalk. The stage stretched out below him, a dizzying drop that he tried not to think about. The catwalks formed a complex web above the stage, disappearing into the shadows.

He moved cautiously, the metal grating beneath his feet creaking softly. The footsteps were closer now, just around the corner of a large set piece suspended from the rigging.

Finn pressed himself against the wall and listened. The footsteps grew louder, more hurried. Just as the figure came around the corner, Finn launched himself forward.

They went down in a tangle of limbs, Finn using his momentum to pin the man to the catwalk. The grating rattled ominously beneath them.

"Don't move!" Finn said, struggling to keep the man pinned. "You're under arrest!"

The man beneath him wheezed, the wind knocked out of him by the fall. "What the hell?" he gasped. "Get off me!"

Finn tightened his grip. "Sheila!" he called out. "I've got him! Up here on the catwalk!"

He heard movement below, then Sheila's voice. "Finn? Where are you?"

"Above the stage!" Finn replied, still struggling with his captive.

There was a pause, then the sound of a door opening. Sheila stepped out onto the stage below, her face upturned and clearly visible in the work lights. She was breathing heavily, hands on her hips.

"Finn," she called up, her voice a mix of confusion and frustration, "the suspect got away. I lost him in the back alley. He had a bike parked there—took off before I could catch up."

Finn froze, the implications of her words sinking in. He looked down at the man he was restraining, really seeing him for the first time. The man glared back, his face red with exertion and anger.

If this wasn't the guy Sheila had been chasing, then who was he?

***

Finn's heart was still racing as he sat across from the man he'd tackled, now identified as Marcus Holloway. They were in one of the theater's dressing rooms, its walls lined with mirrors and bright lights. The juxtaposition of the glamorous space and the tense atmosphere wasn't lost on Finn.

Holloway, a man in his late forties with salt-and-pepper hair and an actor's resonant voice, leaned forward in his chair. "Look, I understand you were just doing your job, but was it really necessary to tackle me like that?"

Finn exchanged a glance with Sheila before responding. "We apologize for the misunderstanding, Mr. Holloway. We're investigating a serious crime, and when I heard someone running above me—"

"You assumed the worst," Holloway said, rubbing his shoulder where he'd hit the catwalk. "I get it. But I'd appreciate an explanation. What exactly is going on in my theater?"

Sheila took the lead. "That's what we're trying to figure out, Mr. Holloway. Can you tell us what you were doing here so late?"

Holloway sighed, running a hand through his disheveled hair. "I was working late, as I often do. We're in the middle of renovations for our upcoming season. I was up in the flies, checking on some new rigging we've installed."

"Renovations?" Finn asked, curious. "What kind of renovations?"

"Oh, a bit of everything," Holloway replied. "We're updating the lighting system, reinforcing some of the older structures, and revamping some of the unused areas. This old place has a lot of hidden nooks and crannies that haven't seen use in decades."

Finn made a mental note of this.

"And you were alone?" Sheila asked.

Holloway nodded. "Yes, I often work late by myself. It's peaceful, gives me time to think and plan without interruptions." He paused, frowning. "At least, I *thought* I was alone. When I heard the commotion, I was trying to figure out what was going on. That's why I was running."

"Did you see anyone else?" Finn asked. "A man, perhaps? Medium build, dark clothes?"

Holloway shook his head. "No, I didn't see anyone. Should I have?"

Finn and Sheila shared another look. Sheila nodded slightly, and Finn turned back to Holloway.

Mr. Holloway," Finn said, leaning forward, his expression grave, "we have reason to believe that someone involved with your theater may be the Coldwater Confessor. We need information on all the actors and anyone else who has access to the theater."

Holloway's face paled, his eyes widening in shock. "The Coldwater Confessor? Here? But that's...that's impossible. I know everyone who works here. They're like family."

"We understand this is difficult to hear, Mr. Holloway," Sheila said, "but we need your cooperation. Any information you can provide could be crucial to our investigation."

Holloway nodded slowly, still visibly shaken. "Of course, of course. I'll get you everything we have—employee records, schedules, access logs. Anything you need."

Just as Finn was about to respond, Sheila's phone buzzed insistently in her pocket. She pulled it out, frowning at the screen. "Excuse me, I need to take this," she said, stepping away from the group.

"Stone," she answered, his voice low.

As she listened, her expression darkened. Finn watched her intently, recognizing the shift in her demeanor. She was on the phone for only a few moments. Then she ended the call and turned back to them, her face grim.

"We have to go," she said to Finn, then addressed Holloway. "Mr. Holloway, we'll be in touch about those records. Please don't discuss this conversation with anyone for now."

Holloway nodded numbly as Finn and Sheila made their way to the door. Once outside, Finn turned to Sheila, puzzled.

"What's going on?" he asked.

Sheila's jaw was set, her voice tight as she spoke. "Another body, that's what."

CHAPTER TWENTY TWO

Sheila's hands gripped the steering wheel tightly as she navigated the empty streets of Coldwater. The clock on the dashboard read 11:48 PM, but she felt wide awake, adrenaline coursing through her veins. Finn sat beside her, his face illuminated by the glow of his phone as he scrolled through the preliminary report on their latest victim.

Another young woman, another life cut short. The weight of responsibility pressed down on her shoulders, threatening to crush her.

They turned onto Maple Street, and Sheila's stomach clenched at the sight of the flashing police lights up ahead. The quiet residential area had been transformed into a bustling crime scene, with uniformed officers milling about and neighbors in bathrobes watching from their porches.

As Sheila parked the car, she took a deep breath, steeling herself for what lay ahead. She'd seen death before, more times than she cared to count, but it never got easier. Each victim was a person with dreams and loves and a future that had been brutally snatched away.

"You ready?" Finn asked softly.

Sheila nodded, her jaw set with determination. "Let's do this."

They ducked under the yellow crime scene tape, flashing their badges at the officer standing guard. The front yard of a modest two-story house was bathed in harsh floodlights, casting long shadows across the manicured lawn.

Sheriff Hank Dawson stood on the front porch, his normally jovial face drawn and pale. As Sheila and Finn approached, she could see the slight tremor in his hands as he clutched his coffee cup.

"Sheriff," Sheila said. "What have we got?"

Dawson took a shaky breath. "It's bad, Stone. Real bad. I've never seen anything like it."

His words sent a chill down Sheila's spine. Dawson was a veteran cop, not easily shaken. If this scene had rattled him...

"Mind taking us through it?" Finn asked.

Dawson nodded, visibly pulling himself together. "Victim is Emily Davis, twenty-eight years old. Neighbor called it in. Said she saw a strange figure leaving the house and went over to check on Emily. That's when she found, well..." He trailed off, his eyes haunted.

"Did the neighbor get a good look at the figure?" Finn asked.

Dawson shook his head. "Not really—it was too dark. But that was part of what made it suspicious: He didn't turn on the porch light, and when he got to his vehicle down the road, he drove away without even turning the headlights on."

He held up a hand, as if predicting Finn's next question. "And no, she didn't get a good look at the vehicle, either. She thought it could've been an SUV, but she wasn't sure."

Finn nodded, but it was clear from the look on his face he was disappointed.

Sheila placed a comforting hand on Dawson's shoulder. "We'll take it from here, Sheriff. Why don't you get some air?"

As Dawson retreated, Sheila and Finn entered the house. The interior was a stark contrast to the peaceful exterior. The entryway was a chaos of overturned furniture and shattered picture frames. A trail of blood led from the living room to the kitchen.

Sheila's eyes followed the trail, her heart heavy with the knowledge of what she'd find at its end. The kitchen was brightly lit, emphasizing the horror of the scene. Emily Davis lay crumpled on the floor, her red hair matted with blood.

Dr. Jin Zihao, the county coroner, looked up as they entered. "Deputies," he said solemnly.

"What can you tell us, Doc?" Finn asked.

Zihao gestured to the body. "Cause of death appears to be blunt force trauma to the head and upper body. Multiple impacts, suggesting a frenzied attack. Weapon was likely cylindrical, possibly a—"

"Candlestick," Sheila finished, her voice tight. Just like the others.

Zihao nodded. "Preliminary time of death is between nine-thirty and ten-thirty pm. I'll know more after the autopsy."

As Zihao continued his examination, Sheila began to survey the room. Her trained eye picked out details others might miss. A broken necklace lay near the victim's hand, its crystal pendant glinting under the harsh lights. A half-empty mug of tea sat on the counter, still faintly warm to the touch.

"She let him in," Sheila murmured. "There's no sign of forced entry. She knew her killer, or he found some way to gain her trust."

Finn nodded. "If he was in disguise..."

Sheila's gaze fell on a corkboard hanging on the wall. It was covered in colorful flyers and business cards. 'New Age Healing Center,' one proclaimed. 'Aura Readings by Madame Zara,' said another.

"Finn, look at this," she said. "Looks like Emily was into New Age spirituality."

"Laura and Sophie were devout, Rachel was an atheist, and now we learn Emily was New Age," Finn murmured. "Maybe religion has nothing to do with it."

As they examined the board, a soft voice spoke from behind them. "She was always searching for meaning."

Sheila turned to see a young woman standing in the doorway, her eyes red-rimmed from crying. "I'm sorry, you are...?"

"Lisa Pritchard," the woman replied. "I'm...I was Emily's best friend. The officers said I could come in to answer some questions."

Sheila nodded, gesturing for Lisa to take a seat at the kitchen table, carefully positioning her away from the gruesome scene on the floor. "Can you tell us about Emily?"

Lisa took a shaky breath. "Em was...she was amazing. So full of life, you know? Always looking for the beauty in everything. That's why she loved working at the gallery."

"And her interest in New Age beliefs?" Finn asked. "When did that start?"

"Oh, that." Lisa gave a watery chuckle. "Em was always exploring different spiritual paths. Said she was looking for her 'true calling.' Last month it was crystals, before that it was tarot cards. She was curious about everything. Sometimes led to some...*interesting* conversations with visitors at the gallery."

"What do you mean by 'interesting'?" Sheila asked.

Lisa shrugged. "Well, you know how art can be. People see different things in it. Emily loved discussing interpretations with visitors, especially if they had a spiritual or mystical bent to them. She'd talk for hours about the energy she felt from certain paintings or sculptures."

Finn leaned forward slightly. "Did she ever mention any particular visitors who shared her interests? Maybe someone who came by frequently?"

Lisa furrowed her brow, thinking. "There were a few regulars, but no one stands out. Oh, wait—there was this one guy. Came in a couple of times last month. Emily said he had some fascinating theories about sacred geometry in art."

Sheila's pulse quickened. "Can you describe this man?"

"I never met him myself," Lisa admitted. "Emily just mentioned him in passing. Said he was middle-aged, kind of intense. But that describes half the art enthusiasts who come through the gallery, to be honest."

Sheila nodded, trying to hide her disappointment. Another vague description, another potential lead that seemed to fade away as soon as they grasped it.

"Did Emily ever mention feeling uncomfortable or threatened by anyone?" Finn asked. "At the gallery or in her personal life?"

Lisa shook her head emphatically. "No, never. Emily was...she was a light, you know? She saw the good in everyone. Even when people were rude or dismissive at the gallery, she'd just say they were having a bad day and try to cheer them up."

Sheila exchanged a glance with Finn. Emily's open, trusting nature might have made her an easy target for their killer.

"One last question, Lisa," Sheila said. "Did Emily mention any new spiritual practices or beliefs recently? Anything out of the ordinary for her?"

Lisa thought for a moment. "Not really. I mean, she was always trying new things, but nothing stood out. Last time we talked, she was excited about some meditation techniques she'd learned. Said they were helping her connect with her 'higher self' or something like that."

Sheila nodded, realizing they weren't going to get any new leads from this conversation. "Thank you, Lisa. You've been very helpful. If you think of anything else, anything at all, please don't hesitate to call us."

As Lisa left, Sheila felt a wave of frustration wash over her. They were no closer to understanding why Emily had been targeted or how she connected to the other victims. The Coldwater Confessor's motives remained as opaque as ever.

"What's going on in your mind?" Finn asked, his voice low.

Sheila shook her head, frustration evident in every line of her body. "I don't know, Finn. I can't see the pattern. The only things connecting Emily to the others are her age and gender. It's like...it's like he's changing his MO."

"Or we never really understood it in the first place," Finn suggested.

Sheila's heart sank. Had they been wrong all along? Were they chasing shadows while the real killer slipped through their fingers?

Finn must have noticed her reaction, because he shook his head regretfully. "I shouldn't have said that," he said, touching her arm. "We'll find him, Sheila, one way or the other. Don't start doubting yourself now."

Sheila nodded, but she didn't take any consolation from his words. She felt like she was drifting, lost in a sea of conflicting evidence and dead ends.

"I can't help but feel like I'm failing, Finn," she said quietly, her voice barely above a whisper. "Four women are dead. Four lives cut short, and we're no closer to catching this bastard than we were when we started."

She ran a hand through her hair, frustration evident in every movement. "I keep thinking about their families, about the fear spreading through Coldwater. People are looking to us for answers, for protection, and what do we have to show for it? Nothing but more bodies and more questions."

Finn started to speak, but Sheila held up a hand, stopping him. "I know what you're going to say. That we're doing our best that these things take time. But every minute we spend chasing our tails is another minute the killer has to plan his next move."

She looked around the crime scene, her eyes lingering on the shattered remnants of Emily's life. "I can't shake the feeling that I'm missing something obvious. That if I were a better detective, a better leader, we'd have caught him by now."

The weight of her perceived failure seemed to physically pull her down, her shoulders slumping. "I need some air," she said abruptly. "I need...I need to clear my head."

"Sheila, wait—" Finn started, but she was already moving.

"I just need some space, Finn," she called over her shoulder. "I'll be back soon."

With that, Sheila walked off into the night, haunted by the ghosts of the past.

CHAPTER TWENTY THREE

As Sheila walked, she pulled out her phone, her fingers hovering over her dad's number. She needed to hear his voice, to draw strength from his unwavering support. But when she dialed, it went straight to voicemail.

Hey, this is Gabriel Stone. Leave a message, and I'll get back to you as soon as I can.

Sheila listened to her father's gruff voice, finding a small measure of comfort in its familiar cadence. She thought about leaving a message but decided against it. What could she say? That she was failing? That she needed help? She ended the call without speaking.

As she continued her aimless wandering, Coldwater seemed to transform around her. The quaint storefronts and familiar landmarks took on a sinister aspect in the late-night gloom. Shadows lengthened, reaching out like grasping fingers. Every alley could be hiding a killer, every darkened window concealing a victim.

Guilt gnawed at her insides. Four women were dead, and she felt responsible for each one. If she'd been smarter, faster, better, maybe they'd still be alive. She'd been so close to catching the killer at the theater, but she'd squandered that opportunity.

Her thoughts drifted to Natalie, as they often did in moments of self-doubt. Her older sister, always so confident, so sure of her path. Until she wasn't. Until the darkness took her. Sheila's heart clenched as she remembered finding Natalie that day, too late to save her.

"I'm sorry, Nat," she whispered into the night. "I'm sorry I couldn't save you. I'm sorry I wasn't strong enough."

Lost in her thoughts, Sheila almost walked past the bar. The neon sign flickered weakly, casting a sickly glow on the sidewalk. She knew she shouldn't go in. Her history with alcohol was a demon she'd fought hard to overcome. But the promise of oblivion, of a brief respite from the crushing weight of her guilt, was too tempting to resist.

The bar was nearly empty, just a few late-night stragglers nursing their drinks in dark corners. Sheila took a seat at the bar, the familiar smell of stale beer and whiskey bringing back a flood of memories, both good and bad.

The bartender, a middle-aged man with kind eyes, approached her. "Rough night?" he asked, his voice sympathetic.

Sheila nodded, not trusting herself to speak.

"What can I get you?"

Sheila's hands clenched on the bar top. She shouldn't be here. She shouldn't do this. But Natalie's face swam before her eyes, accusing, disappointed.

"I...I don't know," she stammered.

The bartender studied her for a moment. "How about we start with some water? You look like you could use a moment to think."

Sheila nodded gratefully, accepting the glass of water he placed before her. As she sipped, the bartender kept a discreet eye on her, seeming to sense her internal struggle.

"Want to talk about it?" he offered after a while.

Sheila looked up, meeting his gaze. She saw no judgment there, just genuine concern. For a moment, she was tempted to pour out everything: the case, her fears, and her guilt. But she held back. He was a total stranger, and besides, he had his own life to worry about without hearing all her problems.

She decided to keep things vague. "Just...having a hard time," she said finally. "Feeling like I'm letting people down."

The bartender nodded sympathetically. "We all feel that way sometimes. The important thing is not to let it consume you."

Sheila's eyes drifted to the row of bottles behind the bar. Each label seemed to call out to her, promising a temporary escape from the crushing weight of her guilt and failure. Her fingers twitched, muscle memory from countless nights spent seeking solace at the bottom of a glass.

She could almost taste the burn of whiskey on her tongue, feel the warmth spreading through her chest as the alcohol dulled her senses. It would be so easy to give in, to let the familiar numbness wash over her.

The sound of the door opening behind her made Sheila tense. For a moment, she was sure it would be Finn coming to pull her back from the brink. Part of her hoped it was him, someone to stop her from making this mistake.

But when she glanced over her shoulder, it was just a stranger—a middle-aged man in a rumpled suit, perhaps coming in for a nightcap after a long day at the office. Sheila turned back to the bar as the reality dawned on her: nobody was coming to save her.

This decision was hers alone.

The bartender had moved away to serve the new customer, leaving Sheila alone with her thoughts and temptations. Her eyes fell on the TV mounted in the corner of the bar, its volume low but captions scrolling across the screen.

Suddenly, a familiar face appeared: Emily Davis, her photo smiling out at the world, unaware of the tragic fate that awaited her. The news ticker beneath announced, 'Fourth victim found in Coldwater Confessor case. Police have no leads.'

The words hit Sheila like a physical blow. No leads. They had nothing. *She* had nothing. Four women dead, and she was no closer to catching the killer than when they started.

In that moment, the last of Sheila's resolve crumbled. She raised her hand, catching the bartender's attention as he returned.

"I'll have a whiskey," she said, her voice hoarse. "Double. Neat."

His eyes crinkled with concern. "You sure about that?"

"Positive. Pour."

As the bartender reached for a bottle, Sheila felt a mix of relief and self-loathing wash over her. She was giving in, falling back into old habits. But at least, for a little while, she might be able to forget her failures.

The glass clinked on the bar in front of her, the amber liquid catching the low light. Sheila stared at it, her hand trembling slightly as she reached out. One drink. Just one to take the edge off. To help her forget, if only for a moment, the weight of her responsibilities and the faces of the women she had failed.

Just one drink.

She lifted the glass, the smell of the whiskey filling her nostrils, bringing with it a flood of memories—some good, many bad. As she brought it to her lips, Sheila closed her eyes, torn between desire and guilt, between the need for escape and the knowledge of where this path could lead.

Just one drink, she told herself again as the liquid spilled like fire across her tongue.

***

Sheila's head throbbed as consciousness slowly returned. She felt herself being lowered onto something soft—a bed? Panic surged through her foggy mind. Where was she? What had happened?

Her eyes snapped open, vision blurry but registering a male figure looming over her. Instinct took over. She lashed out, her fist connecting with something solid.

The man grunted as he stumbled back, raising a hand to his jaw. "Shit, Sheila," he said. "Quite a way to say thank you."

The familiar voice cut through her panic. Sheila blinked rapidly, her surroundings coming into focus. She was in her own bedroom, and the man she'd just struck was indeed her partner, Finn, who was now rubbing his jaw ruefully.

"Finn?" she croaked, her voice hoarse. "What...what happened?"

Finn sighed, sitting on the edge of the bed. "I found you at O'Malley's Bar. You were...pretty out of it. I brought you home."

The events of the night came crashing back, bringing with them a wave of shame. The bar. The whiskey. Breaking her promise to Finn that neither of them would go back to drinking.

She groaned, covering her face with her hands. "Finn, I'm so sorry. I didn't mean to...I just…"

"Hey," Finn said, gently pulling her hands away from her face. "It's okay. We all have moments of weakness."

Sheila shook her head, wincing at the movement. "No, it's not okay. We promised each other, Finn. After everything we've been through, we swore we wouldn't drink anymore. And I just...I threw that away."

She could see the concern in Finn's eyes, mixed with something else. Disappointment? Understanding? She couldn't tell, and that uncertainty only added to her shame.

"How did you find me?" she asked, partly to change the subject and partly out of genuine curiosity.

Finn ran a hand through his hair, looking tired. "When you didn't come back to the crime scene, I got worried. Started checking the places I thought you might go. O'Malley's was my third stop."

Sheila felt a fresh wave of guilt. While she'd been drowning her sorrows, Finn had been out looking for her, probably worried sick.

"I'm sorry," she said again, her voice barely above a whisper. "For making you worry. For breaking our promise. For...for everything."

Finn was quiet for a moment, then reached out and squeezed her hand. "We'll talk about it later, okay? Right now, you need to rest. We've got a killer to catch, and I need my partner at her best."

As he stood to leave, Sheila caught his arm. "Finn...thank you. For finding me. For bringing me home."

He nodded, a small smile on his face. "Always, partner. Now, get some sleep. I'll be back in a few hours with coffee and aspirin."

As the door closed behind him, Sheila sank back into her pillows, her head pounding and her heart heavy. She'd let herself down, let Finn down, and let the whole investigation down.

"Finn, wait," she called out, surprising herself.

The door opened again, and Finn poked his head in. "Yeah?"

"Can you...can you stay? Just for a little while?"

Finn's expression softened. He came back into the room, closing the door behind him. He sat on the edge of the bed, close enough that Sheila could feel the warmth radiating from him.

"Of course," he said, reaching out to take her hand. His touch sent a small shiver through her.

They sat in silence for a moment. Finally, Sheila spoke.

"I can't believe I did that: breaking our promise, disappearing on you...for not being strong enough."

Finn squeezed her hand gently. "Hey, look at me," he said. Sheila raised her eyes to meet his, seeing not judgment but understanding. "You're strong, Sheila. Stronger than you know."

"I don't feel strong," she admitted. "I feel like I'm falling apart."

Finn shifted closer, wrapping an arm around her shoulders. Sheila leaned into him, allowing herself to draw comfort from his presence.

"We all have moments of weakness," he said softly. "What matters is how we pick ourselves up afterward. And you, Sheila Stone, have always been a fighter."

Sheila felt tears prickling at the corners of her eyes. "I don't know if I can do this, Finn. The case, us...everything feels so overwhelming."

Finn's arm tightened around her. "You can do this. *We* can do this. Together." He paused, then continued, his voice thick with emotion. "I love you, Sheila. Not just the perfect, put-together detective, but all of you. The strong parts, the vulnerable parts, all of it."

It wasn't the first time Sheila had heard him say those words, but they were still potent nonetheless. A pleasant feeling spread over her like a warm blanket on a winter's night.

She turned to face him, their faces inches apart. "Finn, I..." Overwhelmed by emotion, she closed the distance between them, pressing her lips to his. The kiss was soft at first, then deepened, conveying everything she couldn't put into words. When they finally pulled apart, both slightly breathless, Sheila felt a newfound strength coursing through her.

"Thank you," she whispered, resting her forehead against his. "For everything."

Finn smiled, brushing a strand of hair from her face. "Always. Now, how about we both get some rest? We've got a killer to catch, and I need my brilliant partner at her best."

Sheila closed her eyes, promising herself that when she woke up, she'd face her mistakes and get back on track. The Coldwater Confessor was still out there, and hungover or not, she had a job to do.

Assuming you're the right person to do it, a voice whispered in the back of her head.

Sheila's eyes snapped open, the thought hitting her like a bucket of ice water. *Was* she the right person? After her lapse, after all the dead ends and missed opportunities, could she really trust herself to lead this investigation?

She tried to sit up straighter, ignoring the pounding in her head. The room spun for a moment before settling.

"Easy," Finn said. "Just rest, okay? You're exhausted."

"I…" Sheila fell silent as she caught her own reflection in the mirror across the room. The woman looking back at her seemed like a stranger: eyes bloodshot, hair disheveled, a shadow of the confident person she'd once been.

You're falling apart, the voice continued. *How can you catch a killer when you can't even stay sober?*

Sheila shook her head, trying to dispel the negative thoughts. But they clung to her like a shroud, whispering doubts and fears. She thought of the victims: Laura, Sophie, Rachel, Emily. They deserved justice. They deserved a detective who was at the top of her game, not someone drowning in self-doubt and guilt.

And then there was Natalie. Her sister's face swam before her eyes, both the vibrant woman she'd been and the broken creature Sheila had found that fateful day. The failure of not being able to save her own sister had pressed down on her for months, and now she felt its full weight in a way she hadn't since discovering her sister's body.

"What is it?" Finn murmured. "What are you thinking about?"

Sheila took a deep breath, her eyes meeting Finn's in the dim light of her bedroom. "I...I don't know if I can do this anymore," she said.

Finn's brow furrowed with concern. "What do you mean?"

"This case, being a detective...all of it," Sheila said, the words tumbling out. "I keep second-guessing myself, blaming myself for not being good enough. For Natalie, for these victims...I'm not sure I have what it takes anymore."

Finn shifted closer, taking her hand in his. "Sheila, listen to me," he said. "You are one of the best detectives I've ever known. Your instincts, your dedication, your heart—that's what makes you great at what you do."

Sheila shook her head, tears threatening to spill. "But I keep failing. Natalie, these women...I couldn't save them."

"You can't save everyone," Finn said softly. "But you can fight for justice for them. And that's exactly what you're doing." He paused, squeezing her hand. "You know, when I first met you, I was in awe of your determination. You never gave up, no matter how tough things got. That fire is still in you, Sheila. I see it every day."

Sheila looked up at him, a glimmer of hope in her eyes. "You really think so?"

Finn nodded, a small smile on his face. "I know so. You're stronger than you realize, Sheila Stone. And you're not alone in this fight. I'm here every step of the way."

His words washed over her, carrying away some of the darkness that had been clouding her mind. Sheila leaned into him, drawing strength from his presence.

"Thank you," she whispered. "For believing in me, even when I don't believe in myself."

Finn wrapped an arm around her, pulling her close. "Always," he said. "Now, what do you say we get some rest, and tomorrow we hit this case with everything we've got?"

As they settled back onto the bed, Finn's arms around her, a sense of peace came over Sheila. The doubts and guilt weren't gone, but they no longer seemed insurmountable. With Finn by her side and a renewed sense of purpose, she was ready to face whatever challenges lay ahead.

The Coldwater Confessor was still out there, but Sheila Stone was back in the game. And this time, she wasn't facing her demons alone.

CHAPTER TWENTY FOUR

The office was already bustling with activity when Sheila and Fin arrived, officers and detectives working overtime on the Coldwater Confessor case. The air was thick with tension and the smell of stale coffee.

Sheila made her way to her desk, ignoring the curious glances from her colleagues. She knew she looked rough, but their opinions were the least of her concerns right now.

Finn was right behind her. The only hint of his long night was his five o'clock shadow.

"Oh," he said with a sigh. "I forgot to mention I did some research last night, looked into the Masquerade Theater—actors, employees, and so on."

"Find anything?"

He shook his head. "Couldn't come up with a promising suspect. If that really was the killer there, he's kept his interest in theater low-key."

Sheila sat down heavily in her chair, pulling the nearest stack of files toward her. "Then we're back to the basics," she said. "Let's review everything. There's gotta be something we missed."

Finn grunted. "This is the fun stuff they don't tell you about in the academy. You go in thinking it's all about drug busts and foot chases. Turns out, most bad guys are caught on paper."

"Just so long as he's caught," Sheila murmured.

It didn't take long for Sheila's eyes to begin to burn as she pored over witness statements, autopsy reports, and crime scene photos. The faces of the victims stared back at her from their files: Laura, Sophie, Rachel, Emily. Four women whose lives had been cut short, four families left devastated. Sheila felt the weight of their expectations, their need for justice, pressing down on her.

As she reviewed her notes from their interview with Lisa Pritchard, Emily Davis's friend, something Lisa had said jumped out at her: 'Emily had some...*interesting* conversations with visitors at the gallery.'

Sheila sat up straight, her sudden movement catching Finn's attention. "What is it?" he asked.

"Something Lisa said about Emily having religious conversations at the art gallery," Sheila murmured. "It goes along with what Sophie's roommate said—how Sophie had talked with someone about unusual religious ideas before she died."

Finn frowned, leaning in to look at the file. "You think there's a connection?"

"Maybe," Sheila said, pursing her lips in thought. She stood up, moved to the whiteboard, and began creating a timeline. "What if our killer isn't just targeting random women? What if he's choosing victims based on their reaction to his beliefs?"

Finn leaned back, picking up an old baseball off his desk and tossing it in the air. "So you think he's approaching these women, trying to convert them to his...what, his personal religion? And when they reject him—"

"He kills them," Sheila finished grimly. "It fits with the religious overtones we've seen in his letter and the crime scenes."

"What about Laura Hastings and Rachel Kim? Where are the connections with them?"

"I don't know. It's not like we can figure out every single person they spoke with in the days leading up to their deaths. But it fits, Finn. It explains so much."

Finn said nothing. Sheila had the impression he was keeping silent for fear of discouraging her. He had his doubts, but he didn't want to pour cold water on her enthusiasm.

"Assuming you're on the right track," Finn said, "where does this lead? Do we head over to the art gallery, try to figure out who Emily spoke with?"

"That's one option."

He arched an eyebrow. "Which is your way of saying it's not what *you'd* choose to do, right?"

"I think we should look into any new or unusual religious groups in Coldwater," Sheila said, pacing the room. "Anything that's popped up in the last year or so."

Finn nodded, staring off into space for a few seconds as if mentally shifting gears. Then he cleared his throat and sat up straighter. "Alright," he said as he reached for his phone. "I'll check with the local churches, see if they've noticed any new faces or strange behavior."

As Finn made his calls, Sheila dove into online research. She scrolled through local forums, social media groups, and community bulletin boards, looking for any mention of new spiritual movements or unusual religious gatherings. The more she searched, the more convinced she became that they were on the right track.

"Reverend Adams says they've had a few new faces at Sunday services," Finn said, hanging up the phone. "But nothing that stands out as suspicious. No one pushing strange ideologies or cornering people after the service."

Sheila nodded, only half-listening as she continued her online search. She was about to move on to another forum when a small ad caught her eye. It was for a group called 'The Celestial Awakening,' promising enlightenment and spiritual transcendence. The language used was eerily similar to some of the phrases in the Coldwater Confessor's letters.

"Finn," she called out, "I think I've got something."

As Finn came over, Sheila pulled up more information about the group. It was small, only a dozen or so members, and had been meeting for about six months.

"Any names jump out at you?" Finn asked, leaning in to look at the screen.

Sheila pointed to a few names. "David Larson, he's a local real estate agent. No criminal record, but he's been through two messy divorces. Could be harboring resentment toward women."

Finn shook his head. "Nah, I know Dave. He's a bit of a jerk, but he doesn't fit our profile. Who else?"

"Meredith Hale," Sheila continued. "She's new in town, moved here about eight months ago. Not much background on her."

"A woman?" Finn raised an eyebrow. "Possible, but doesn't fit with the descriptions of the killer. I know he wears disguises, but he'd have to be one hell of an actor for that."

Sheila nodded, scrolling further down the list. Suddenly, her finger stopped on a name. "Wait a minute. Ezra Thorne. That name rings a bell."

Finn's brow furrowed as he thought. "Ezra Thorne...didn't we see his name at that prop store?"

"Spotlight Costumes? Yeah, he was on that poster. The one for the theater." Her heart rate kicked up a notch as she looked up more information about Ezra Thorne on her laptop. It wasn't difficult to find articles from the Masquerade Theater group, one of which described Thorne as a 'set designer.'

"I've got his social media here," Finn said, scrolling through his phone. "Forty-two moved to Coldwater about a year ago. Big into acting. He could be the one that was staying in that hidden room in the theater."

Sheila nodded, a surge of adrenaline coursing through her. "And look at this—he's listed as the group leader for tonight's meeting of the Celestial Awakening."

Finn leaned back in his chair, processing the information. "It fits, Sheila. The theater connection, the timing of his arrival in Coldwater, his position in this new religious group. This could be our guy."

"We need to get to that meeting," Sheila said, already reaching for her jacket. "If Thorne is our killer, this might be our best chance to catch him in the act."

"Hold on," Finn cautioned, grabbing her arm. "We can't just barge in there. If we're wrong, we could blow the whole investigation. And if we're right, we could be walking into a room full of his followers."

Sheila paused, considering. "You're right. We need to be smart about this. We'll go undercover, pose as interested newcomers. We can observe Thorne, see how he interacts with the group, maybe even get him talking about his beliefs."

"This is a small town, Sheila. There's a decent chance someone might recognize us. We're not exactly strangers around here."

Sheila considered this for a moment, then shook her head. "I'm not too worried about that. Think about it—most of the people who'd recognize us are upstanding citizens who wouldn't be mixed up in something like this. Plus, the group's only been around for six months. Chances are, the members are mostly newcomers to town or people who keep to themselves."

"Maybe," Finn said, though he still looked uncertain.

"It's a risk we have to take," Sheila said. "Besides, people see what they expect to see. No one's going to be looking for two cops at a spiritual meeting. As long as we play our parts well, we should be fine."

Finn's expression cleared, and he nodded. "So what's our cover story?"

"We'll be a couple interested in spiritual enlightenment," Sheila said, a grim smile forming on her face. "New to town, looking for meaning in our lives."

"And if we confirm thorne's our guy..." Finn said.

"We take him down," Sheila finished. "Quietly, without tipping off the rest of the group if possible."

Their eyes met, and Sheila could see the same mixture of excitement and determination she felt reflected in Finn's gaze.

"It's time we rip off his mask," she said.

CHAPTER TWENTY FIVE

Sheila felt a strange mixture of excitement and unease as she and Finn approached the community center. It wasn't often she went undercover, and she was keenly aware of how easily things could go wrong. If Ezra Thorne really was the killer, there was no telling how he would react to being confronted.

Nor what the other Celestial Awakening members might do if they were present when that confrontation happened.

They'd dressed casually—Sheila in jeans and a loose blouse, Finn in khakis and a polo shirt—trying to blend in with the crowd they expected at the meeting. They didn't know whether this group ever got walk-ins, but if all else failed, they could always pretend they were lost and looking for directions.

The building was an unremarkable brick structure, its windows glowing warmly in the gathering dusk. A simple sign by the entrance read "The Celestial Awakening—All Welcome." Sheila couldn't help but think of the irony: how unwelcome she and Finn would be if their true identities were discovered.

"Remember," Finn murmured as they neared the entrance, his breath visible in the cool air, "we're just a couple interested in spiritual enlightenment. Keep it low-key."

Sheila nodded, taking a deep breath to calm her nerves. She could feel the weight of her concealed weapon against her hip, a constant reminder of the danger they might be walking into. With one last shared glance, they pushed open the doors and stepped inside.

The community center's lobby was bustling with activity. People of all ages milled about, some chatting animatedly, others looking as nervous as Sheila felt. A table near the entrance was stacked with pamphlets and sign-up sheets. Sheila grabbed one, noting the elaborate celestial designs that bordered the text.

They made their way to the meeting room, Sheila's eyes constantly scanning their surroundings, taking in every detail. The room was already half-full; people gathered in small groups, their voices a low murmur that filled the space. Sheila's gaze darted from face to face, looking for Ezra Thorne, but he was nowhere to be seen.

"Welcome!" said a cheerful voice, startling Sheila. She turned to see a woman in her forties, her face wreathed in a warm smile. She had kind eyes and graying hair pulled back in a loose bun. "I'm Margaret. Is this your first time with us?"

Sheila forced a smile, hoping it looked genuine. "Yes, we're...exploring new spiritual paths. I'm Sarah, and this is my partner, Frank."

Margaret's eyes lit up, her enthusiasm almost overwhelming. "Oh, how wonderful! You've come to the right place. We believe that the universe is interconnected in ways most people can't even imagine. Our leader, Ezra—he's opened our eyes to the true nature of reality."

Sheila nodded politely, her eyes continuing to scan the room. She noted the exits, the layout of the chairs, the small stage at the front.

"So, how long have you been part of this group?" Finn asked, his voice filled with practiced curiosity.

Margaret beamed. "Oh, I've been with Ezra from the beginning. About six months now. It's been a life-changing experience. I used to feel so lost, you know? But now I understand my place in the cosmic order."

"We're hoping to find the same thing," Finn said.

"Oh, you will—I have no doubt about it. This community is more a family than anything else. We are all united by one great cause despite the many different backgrounds we come from. I firmly believe that everything happens for a reason, and there's no question you were fated to come here. This very conversation we're having now…"

As Margaret continued to drone on about the workings of fate, Sheila's attention was drawn to a man who had just entered the room. He was tall and lean, with salt-and-pepper hair and an aura of quiet authority. People seemed to gravitate toward him, their faces lighting up as he passed.

Suddenly, a hush fell over the crowd. The man had made his way to the front of the room, and Sheila realized with a jolt that this must be Ezra Thorne. In person, he was more imposing than his photo suggested. His piercing blue eyes seemed to look right through you, and there was an intensity to his presence that was almost palpable.

She tried to figure out if he was the same man she'd chased in the theater, but she couldn't be sure. She simply hadn't gotten a good look at the suspect.

"Friends," Thorne said, his rich and resonant voice carrying across the room, "let us begin."

The group moved to form a circle of chairs. Sheila and Finn found seats. As Thorne began to speak, Sheila listened intently, her cop instincts on high alert.

"We are the chosen few," Thorne said, his eyes blazing with intensity, "entrusted with knowledge that could reshape the world. But with this knowledge comes great responsibility. We must be prepared to make sacrifices for the greater good."

Sheila felt a chill run down her spine. She glanced at Finn, seeing her own suspicion mirrored in his eyes. What kind of sacrifices was Thorne talking about? Personal sacrifices…

Or the sacrifice of others?

Thorne's voice rose and fell like a tide, washing over the rapt audience. Sheila found her gaze drawn to his eyes, which seemed to glitter with an inner fire as he spoke.

"The universe whispers its secrets to those who listen," Thorne said, his hands moving in graceful arcs as if conducting an invisible orchestra. "Can you hear it, my friends? The cosmic symphony that plays just beyond the veil of our mundane reality?"

A woman in the front row let out a soft gasp, her eyes wide with wonder. Beside her, a middle-aged man nodded fervently, his lips moving in silent repetition of Thorne's words.

"We are the chosen few," Thorne continued, his voice dropping to a near-whisper that somehow carried to every corner of the room. "Entrusted with knowledge that could reshape the world." He paused, his gaze sweeping across the audience, seeming to make eye contact with each person in turn. When his eyes met Sheila's, she felt a jolt of electricity run down her spine.

"But with this knowledge comes great responsibility," Thorne said, his voice hardening. "We must be prepared to make sacrifices for the greater good."

A murmur rippled through the crowd. Sheila glanced at Finn, noting the slight furrow of his brow. She felt her own unease growing, the word 'sacrifices' echoing ominously in her mind.

Thorne raised his hands, palms up, as if offering something to the heavens. "The cosmic order demands balance," he said. "And those who reject the truth, they are lost to the darkness." His voice grew louder, more intense. "It is our duty to show them the light by any means necessary."

"Yes," breathed the woman in the front row, her eyes shining with unshed tears. Others nodded, their faces masks of determination.

There was something magnetic about Thorne, a charisma that made his words seem profound even when they verged on nonsensical. She could see how people might fall under his spell, might be willing to do anything he asked.

It would explain how he got close to his victims, she thought.

Just then, a commotion near the door caught her attention. A latecomer had arrived, apologizing profusely for his tardiness. As he made his way into the room, Sheila's blood ran cold.

It was a police officer Sheila knew, Officer Michael Johnson. His eyes widened as he spotted Sheila and Finn. His mouth opened in surprise, and before Sheila could signal him to be quiet, he blurted out, "Deputy Stone? Deputy Mercer? What are you—"

The room fell silent. All eyes turned to Sheila and Finn. Sheila could feel the mood shift instantly, curiosity turning to suspicion and then to anger.

So much for no one recognizing us, she thought.

"Police?" someone gasped, the word rippling through the crowd like a shockwave.

Thorne's face darkened, his charismatic mask slipping to reveal something harder, more dangerous beneath. "You dare to infiltrate our sacred gathering?"

Sheila raised her hands in a placating gesture. "Please, everyone, remain calm. We're not here to cause any trouble."

Finn nodded, adding, "We're just here to observe. We have no intention of disrupting your meeting."

But their words fell on deaf ears. The crowd's anger was palpable, a living thing that seemed to fill the room.

Margaret, who had been so welcoming earlier, now looked at them with cold eyes. "You lied to us," she said. "You're not seekers. You're spies!"

"Unbelievers!" someone else shouted from the back of the room.

Sheila tried again to defuse the situation. "We're just doing our job. There's no need for—"

Her words were cut off as a chair came flying through the air, narrowly missing Finn's head. Then a bald man grabbed Finn's jacket from behind, and Finn threw his elbow back, striking the man hard in the face.

The bald man stumbled, pressing a hand to his bloody nose. There was a moment of stunned silence as the group realized what had just happened. Then a floorboard at the back of the room creaked—Thorne was using the commotion as a distraction so he could escape through a back door.

"Go after him!" Finn said to Sheila as he raised his fists. "I'll buy you some time."

"Finn—" she began, not wanting to leave him behind, but he cut her off.

"Go!" he shouted. "He's getting away!"

With a deep breath, Sheila turned and started running.

CHAPTER TWENTY SIX

Sheila pushed past a group of shouting followers, ignoring their grasping hands and angry cries. She burst through the side door and into a dimly lit hallway. Ahead, she could hear the sound of running footsteps echoing off the walls.

Behind her, she could still hear the sounds of the scuffle in the meeting room. She said a silent prayer that Finn would be okay, then focused all her attention on the fleeing suspect ahead. She wasn't going to let him get away again.

The hallway seemed to stretch on forever, twisting and turning through the bowels of the community center. Sheila could hear Thorne just ahead, his breathing heavy, his footsteps echoing off the walls. She pushed herself harder, gaining ground inch by inch.

Suddenly, the hallway opened up into a large storage room. Shelves lined the walls, stacked high with boxes and old furniture. Sheila skidded to a stop, her eyes darting around the space. Where had he gone?

Sheila skidded to a stop, her eyes darting around the space. Where had he gone? The storage room was a maze of shelves and discarded furniture, shadows lurking in every corner. She strained her ears, listening for any sound that might betray Thorne's location.

A faint scuff to her left caught her attention. Sheila spun, catching a glimpse of movement behind a stack of old filing cabinets. She moved carefully, her footsteps silent on the concrete floor.

"Thorne!" she called out, her voice steady despite her racing heart. "There's nowhere to go. Come out now, and we can talk about this."

Silence was her only answer. Sheila inched forward, her hand on her weapon. She needed to be smart about this. Thorne had the advantage of knowing the layout of this room, and she couldn't risk letting him slip past her.

Sheila inched forward, her senses on high alert. The storage room was quiet, the only sound her own controlled breathing. She rounded a corner, peering between two tall shelving units.

Suddenly, a dark figure burst from the shadows. Thorne lunged at her, his face contorted with rage and desperation. Sheila barely had time to react as his body slammed into hers, sending them both crashing to the ground.

They grappled on the dusty floor, Thorne fighting with the strength of a cornered animal. His elbow caught Sheila in the ribs, knocking the wind out of her. For a moment, he had the upper hand, his weight pinning her down.

But Sheila wasn't defenseless. Years of kickboxing training kicked in, muscle memory taking over. She bucked her hips, destabilizing Thorne's position. In one fluid motion, she wrapped her legs around his torso, using the leverage to flip their positions.

Now on top, Sheila drove her knee into Thorne's solar plexus, causing him to gasp and loosen his grip. Taking advantage of his momentary weakness, she grabbed his arm and twisted it behind his back, effectively immobilizing him.

"It's over, Thorne," she said, reaching for her handcuffs. "Stop fighting."

Thorne struggled for a few more seconds before going limp, the fight draining out of him. Sheila quickly secured the handcuffs, her heart still racing from the intense confrontation.

As she hauled Thorne to his feet, something caught her eye. A tuft of hair was sticking out oddly from his scalp. Frowning, Sheila reached out and tugged gently. To her surprise, the entire head of hair came away in her hand.

A wig.

He'd been wearing a disguise—just like Sheila believed the killer did.

***

Hours later, Sheila stood in the observation room, her eyes fixed on Ezra Thorne through the one-way mirror. He sat alone in the interrogation room, his face impassive, hands folded neatly on the table in front of him. His hair—his natural hair, that was—was gray and tangled.

Francine Albright had described the priest as having gray hair, but she'd said it was 'very neat.' This man's hair didn't strike Sheila as neat, but then again, neat was a subjective descriptor. Neat to one person might be messy to someone else.

"What do you think?" Finn asked, coming to stand beside her.

Sheila sighed, running a hand through her hair. "I don't know. It's hard to be certain about anything right now."

Finn raised an eyebrow. "You're having doubts? Sheila, this guy fits the profile perfectly. The religious angle, the connection to the theater, the disguises—it all fits. Not to mention his reaction when we showed up at the meeting."

"I know, I know," Sheila said, trying not to get frustrated. "But what if we're seeing what we want to see? What if we're so desperate for a break in the case that we're forcing the pieces to fit?"

Finn was about to respond when the door to the interrogation room opened. A woman in a sharp suit walked in, her heels clicking on the tile floor. Thorne's attorney had arrived.

"Damn," Finn muttered. "There goes our chance to question him."

Sheila nodded, her brow furrowed in thought. The arrival of the lawyer complicated things. They'd have to wait now, give Thorne time to confer with his attorney. And all the while, a nagging doubt gnawed at the back of Sheila's mind.

What if they were wrong? What if Ezra Thorne, for all his suspicious behavior, wasn't the Coldwater Confessor? The real killer could still be out there, perhaps even planning his next move while they focused on the wrong man.

The door to the observation room burst open, startling both detectives. Sheriff Hank Dawson strode in, his face a mask of barely contained stress.

"Stone, Mercer," he said brusquely. "What's the situation with Thorne?"

"The situation," Finn said, "is that his lawyer just arrived. Could be a while before we get the chance to talk to him."

Dawson glanced at his watch and cursed under his breath. "Damn it. We don't have time for this. The mayor's breathing down my neck, demanding updates. The public is in a panic, and we need to give them something."

"Sir," Sheila said cautiously, "we're not sure yet if Thorne is actually our killer. We need more time to investigate—"

"Time is a luxury we don't have, Stone," Dawson said, cutting her off. "I've scheduled a press conference for an hour from now. I need you and Mercer there to share your findings on the case."

Sheila's eyes widened in disbelief. "An hour? Sheriff, that's not nearly enough time to—"

"It'll have to be," Dawson interrupted again. "People are scared, Stone—they're hiding in their homes, talking about canceling church services. They need reassurance. They need to know we're making progress."

"With all due respect, sir," Finn said, "if we go public with information that turns out to be wrong, it could jeopardize the entire investigation."

Dawson's shoulders sagged, the weight of his responsibility evident in every line of his body. "I understand your concerns. But right now, perception is as important as facts. We need to show the public that we're on top of this, that they can feel safe in their homes again."

Sheila opened her mouth to protest, but Dawson held up a hand. "I've already made my decision," he said. "I suggest you spend the next hour getting ready for what you're going to say."

With that, Dawson left the room. Sheila stared after him, feeling the pressure mounting. She had one hour—one hour to either prove Thorne's guilt beyond a shadow of a doubt or find evidence that exonerated him.

But where to start? The wig was suspicious, but not conclusive. Thorne's behavior at the meeting could be explained by simple paranoia or anti-government sentiment. They needed something solid, something that either tied Thorne definitively to the murders or ruled him out completely.

Sheila's mind raced, reviewing every detail of the case: the victims, the crime scenes, the religious symbolism, the theater connection...

Suddenly, an idea struck her.

"Finn," she said, her voice tight with urgency, "we need to search Thorne's house. If he's our guy, there's a good chance he'll have some candlesticks there, ready for future victims."

Finn frowned. "What if he's run out of candlesticks?"

Sheila took a deep breath, steeling herself for the possibility. "Then we need to be prepared to tell Dawson and the public that we might have the wrong man. And that the Coldwater Confessor could still be out there."

CHAPTER TWENTY SEVEN

Sheila's stomach did somersaults as she pulled up to Ezra Thorne's house. A clock was ticking in the back of her head, counting down the seconds until that press conference. She needed to find something definitive before then, or else there was no telling how much damage that press conference might do.

The modest two-story home sat on a quiet street, its white paint peeling slightly in the late afternoon sun. A well-manicured lawn stretched out front, at odds with the sinister suspicions swirling in Sheila's mind.

"Sheila," Finn said, his voice tight with concern, "we shouldn't be here. We don't have a warrant."

She turned off the engine, her jaw set with determination. "I know, Finn. But we're running out of time. If Thorne has a collection of candlesticks, or even a single one that matches the candlesticks used on the victims, we need to find it before the press conference."

Finn sighed, rubbing his forehead. "Assuming we do find such a candlestick, any evidence we collect here won't be admissible in court. We could blow the whole case."

"We're not collecting evidence," Sheila replied, already opening her door. "We're just...looking. If we find something, we'll get a warrant. Come on."

She could tell Finn still wasn't happy, but he didn't argue further. They approached the front door, and Sheila knocked. To the best of her knowledge, Thorne lived alone, but there was no harm in checking.

No answer.

Sheila tried the handle—locked, as expected. She glanced around, spotting a fake rock near a potted plant.

"Really?" Finn muttered as she lifted it to reveal a key. "That's so cliché."

Sheila shrugged, inserting the key. "Sometimes the classics work best."

The door swung open with a creak, revealing a dimly lit entryway. Sheila stepped inside, her senses on high alert. The house smelled of old books and something herbal—incense, maybe.

"You take the ground floor, I'll go upstairs," she said.

Finn nodded reluctantly, still clearly uncomfortable with the situation. As he moved toward the living room, Sheila climbed the stairs, her footsteps muffled by the thick carpet.

The upper floor was a maze of closed doors. Sheila opened the first one, revealing a sparse guest bedroom. Nothing out of the ordinary caught her eye—just a neatly made bed and a dresser with a few framed photos. She moved on.

The next room was clearly Thorne's study. Bookshelves lined the walls, crammed with tomes on religion, philosophy, and astronomy. A large desk dominated the center of the room, its surface covered in papers filled with complex diagrams and scribbled notes.

Sheila rifled through the drawers, her heart pounding. She found more papers, a few USB drives, but no candlestick. Frustration gnawed at her as she moved to the closet.

Boxes of files, more books, but nothing that could be a murder weapon.

She was about to leave when something caught her eye. A small safe, tucked away in the corner of the closet. Sheila knelt down, examining it closely. There was no keyhole, just a smooth metal surface with an intricate design etched into it.

Her fingers traced the pattern. It looked familiar—a series of interconnected lines and dots. Constellations, she realized. Orion, Cassiopeia, Ursa Major—the same ones mentioned in the Confessor's letters.

Sheila's mind raced. Was this a combination lock? She tried pressing the stars in various sequences, following the mythological stories associated with each constellation. Nothing happened.

Frustration mounting, she sat back on her heels, staring at the safe. There had to be a way in. Her eyes wandered to Thorne's desk, which was covered in astronomical charts and diagrams. Maybe there was a clue there?

She rifled through the papers, her heart pounding with every creak of the old house. A sheet caught her attention—a star chart with certain constellations circled in red. But it wasn't the constellations themselves that interested her. It was the numbers scribbled next to each one.

Sheila rushed back to the safe, hope rising in her chest. She pressed the stars in the sequential order indicated by the numbers. Twenty-one, forty-three, fifty-six, seventy-one…

Nothing.

"Come on," she muttered, trying again. Still nothing.

She was about to give up when a new thought struck her. What if the numbers weren't a sequence, but rather coordinates on the safe's surface? She remembered seeing similar systems in some of Thorne's astronomical writings, where he used a grid system to map out star positions.

With trembling fingers, she tried again. This time, instead of following the numbers in order, she imagined the safe's face as a grid. If the top left corner was zero-zero, then each number pair could represent a specific point on the safe's surface.

The first constellation had the numbers two and one next to it, so she pressed the spot two units to the right and one unit down from the top left corner. She did the same for each constellation, using their respective number pairs to determine where to press.

As she pressed the final point, there was a soft click. The safe door swung open. She let out a sigh of relief. She could hardly believe it had worked.

Inside the safe, she found stacks of cash, some jewelry, and a few old books. But no candlestick. Sheila slammed the safe shut, her frustration mounting.

"All that for nothing," she muttered.

Downstairs, she could hear Finn moving around. She hoped he was having better luck than she was.

The master bedroom was her last hope. It was larger than the guest room, with a king-sized bed and heavy curtains blocking out the afternoon sun. Sheila searched methodically: under the bed, in the nightstands, through the closet. Nothing.

Finn's voice drifted up from below. "Sheila? You need to see this."

She hurried downstairs, finding Finn in the kitchen. He was standing in front of an open pantry, his face pale.

"What is it?" Sheila asked, peering around him.

The pantry was full of canned goods and dry staples, but that's not what had caught Finn's attention. On one shelf, partially hidden behind a box of cereal, was a small bottle of ipecac syrup.

The same substance used to poison Jason Reeves, Rachel Kim's dog sitter.

"Shit," Sheila said.

This was damning evidence, but not what they had come for. And besides, they couldn't take it without a warrant.

"Any candlesticks?" she asked, already knowing the answer.

Finn shook his head. "Nothing. Sheila, we need to go. We've already crossed a line being here. If we're caught..."

She nodded reluctantly. "You're right. Let's go."

As they made their way to the front door, Sheila's mind was whirling. The poison was certainly suspicious, but the absence of even a single candlestick still nagged at her. Had Thorne hidden it well…

Or was its absence proof of his innocence?

***

Sheila's footsteps echoed in the empty hallway of the community center. The building felt different now, devoid of the energy and fervor that had filled it during the Celestial Awakening meeting.

She checked her watch—fifteen minutes until the press conference. Finn was back at the station, probably pacing nervously as he prepared their statement.

And cursing her under his breath.

But Sheila couldn't shake the feeling that they were missing something crucial. That's why she'd come back here, hoping to find...well, she wasn't sure what exactly. A clue, a hint, anything that might point them in the right direction.

As she walked, her mind went over everything they knew about the Coldwater Confessor: the disguises, the priest impersonation, the first murder in the confessional, the candlestick... Each piece of the puzzle seemed to fit Thorne, and yet something felt off.

Sheila paused in front of a bulletin board covered in flyers and announcements. Her eyes scanned the colorful papers absently as her thoughts wandered to the other members of Celestial Awakening. Who were they, really? What had drawn them to Thorne's teachings?

She thought about the victims: Laura, Sophie, Rachel, Emily. Their faces haunted her dreams, their unsolved murders a constant reminder of her failure. And now, with the press conference looming, she felt the pressure more than ever. If they were wrong about Thorne, if the real killer was still out there...

Sheila shook her head, trying to clear the dark thoughts. She had to focus. There had to be something here, some clue they'd overlooked.

She moved on, entering the room where the meeting had been held. Chairs were still arranged in a circle, an echo of the gathering that had ended in chaos. Sheila walked the perimeter slowly, her trained eyes taking in every detail.

A movement caught her attention: a piece of paper fluttering in the breeze from an open window. She approached, realizing it was a photograph that had fallen from a nearby bulletin board. Sheila picked it up, her eyes scanning the image of smiling faces—members of Celestial Awakening at what appeared to be a recent gathering.

Her gaze was drawn to a figure standing next to Thorne. A man, middle-aged with salt-and-pepper hair and intense eyes. Something about him seemed oddly familiar, but Sheila couldn't quite figure out why.

Frowning, she pulled out her phone and began scrolling through Thorne's social media accounts, searching for any mention or tag of this mysterious man. As she delved deeper, her phone buzzed with incoming texts from Finn. She glanced at them briefly—he was getting impatient, reminding her of the impending press conference. Sheila ignored the messages. He'd just have to wait.

Moments ticked by as she scoured Thorne's online presence, frustration mounting as she found no clear connection to the stranger in the photo. She was about to give up when something caught her eye: a comment on an old post mentioning a "Dr. R" who had introduced Thorne to some new ideas.

Suddenly, it clicked. Sheila's mind flashed back to Laura Hastings' house, to a framed photo she'd noticed during their initial investigation. The stranger had been in that picture, standing in the background at what looked like a community event.

With renewed energy, Sheila started searching through Laura's social media accounts. It didn't take long to find what she was looking for: a post thanking 'Dr. Calvin Reeves' for his insights at a fundraising event at the library.

Her heart racing, Sheila dug deeper. Apparently, Dr. Calvin Reeves was a psychiatrist specializing in religious counseling. As she scrolled through his professional page, she found connections to not just Laura, but all four victims. Sophie had attended a workshop he'd led. Rachel had been photographed at a charity event where he was a speaker. And Emily had shared one of his articles just weeks before her death.

Then she came across an obituary for a woman named Helen Reeves—Dr. Reeves's wife. It appeared that, three years ago, she'd been struck by lightning while out for a jog. Had this inspired Dr. Reeves's killings? Had he taken it as some kind of a sign?

The pieces were falling into place. Reeves would have had the opportunity to interact with all the victims, to try and convert them to his beliefs. And when they refused...

She dialed Finn's number, her hands shaking slightly with the intensity of her discovery. As soon as he picked up, she spoke urgently, "Finn, we need to stop that press conference. I think I know who the real Coldwater Confessor is."

CHAPTER TWENTY EIGHT

Dr. Calvin Reeves, known to himself as 'the Father,' stood in the dim room, his face illuminated by the flickering light of candles. The air was thick with the scent of incense, a heady mixture of sandalwood and myrrh that would purify the space for the ritual to come.

He was arranging ceremonial items on a small altar: a silver chalice, a worn Bible, and a candlestick—an instrument of cleansing. He'd always loved rituals, time-honored traditions. It was an ode to the past, to an understanding of the world that predated his lifetime.

Perhaps that was why he enjoyed theater, at least the ones that focused on the classics. Too bad he couldn't go back to the Masquerade any time soon.

His eyes fell on the unconscious form of Megan Philips, bound to a chair in the center of the room. A pang of something—regret? Doubt?—flashed through him, but he quickly suppressed it. This was necessary.

This was his calling, as he had known the moment his wife was killed in that storm. She'd been a distraction, a hindrance. She'd been removed so he could focus solely on his mission.

His mind drifted back to earlier that day, when he had first laid eyes on Megan at his community outreach seminar. She had stood out immediately—bright, articulate, questioning. He had seen the potential in her, the spark that could be nurtured into a blazing faith. But when he'd approached her afterwards, sharing his vision of cosmic truth, she had recoiled. Her rejection stung, and he'd known right away that she had to be punished.

It hadn't been difficult to lure her here. A simple ruse—a dropped wallet, a moment of distraction in the parking lot. The chloroform had done the rest. Now, as he watched her stir, beginning to regain consciousness, he steeled himself for what was to come.

Megan's eyes fluttered open, confusion quickly giving way to fear as she took in her surroundings. "What...where am I? Dr. Reeves? What's going on?"

"Hush, child," the Father said. "You're here for a greater purpose. To be cleansed, to be made worthy of the cosmic truth."

"Cleansed? What are you talking about? Let me go!" Megan struggled against her bonds, panic rising in her voice.

The Father sighed, shaking his head. "I had hoped you would understand, Megan. That you would see the light willingly. But sometimes, the path to enlightenment requires...intervention."

He began to pace, his words flowing with the fervor of a true believer. "You see, Megan, we are at a crucial juncture in the universe's grand design. The stars are aligning, the cosmic forces converging. But for the great awakening to occur, the world must be purified. Those who reject the truth...they are obstacles. Impurities that must be removed."

Megan's eyes widened with horrified realization. "You...you're the one they've been looking for. The Coldwater Confessor. You killed those women!"

"Killed?" The Father's voice rose with indignation. "No, you misunderstand. I saved them. Freed them from their earthly sins, their stubborn rejection of the divine plan. Just as I will save you."

"Dr. Reeves, please," Megan pleaded, her voice shaking. "This isn't you. You're a psychiatrist, you help people. Think about your patients, your colleagues. What would they say if they saw you now?"

For a moment, the Father faltered. Images flashed through his mind: years of study, of counseling troubled souls, of being a respected member of the community. When had it all changed? When had he first heard the cosmic whispers, seen the grand design hidden in the stars?

But as quickly as the doubt came, it was washed away by the certainty of his mission. "They would not understand," he said, more to himself than to Megan. "They are still blind to the truth. But soon, very soon, all will be revealed."

He turned back to the altar, lifting the ornate candlestick. Its weight felt right in his hand, a perfect balance of form and function. "This," he said, holding it up for Megan to see, "is the key to your salvation. Through this, you will be cleansed, your soul freed to join the cosmic dance."

Megan thrashed in her chair, tears streaming down her face. "No, please! You don't have to do this! Whatever you believe, whatever you think is going to happen, this isn't the way!"

The Father approached her, candlestick raised. "I'm sorry you can't see the beauty of it, Megan. But in time, in the great beyond, you'll understand. You'll thank me for this gift."

He began to chant. The candlelight danced across the walls, casting grotesque shadows. Megan's pleas became more desperate, but to the Father, they were merely the death throes of her unenlightened self.

He raised the candlestick higher, ready to deliver the cleansing blow.

CHAPTER TWENTY NINE

Sheila's knuckles were white as she gripped the steering wheel, her police cruiser cutting through the quiet streets of Coldwater. The sun was setting, casting long shadows across the road, but Sheila barely noticed the picturesque scene. Her mind was focused entirely on her destination: Dr. Calvin Reeves' house.

Her phone, on speaker mode and resting on the dashboard, crackled to life with Finn's voice. "Sheila, where the hell are you? The press conference is about to start!"

"It doesn't matter, Finn," she replied, her voice tense. "We can't go through with it. Not now."

"What are you talking about? We've got Thorne in custody. The mayor, the chief, everyone's waiting—"

"Thorne isn't our killer," Sheila said, cutting him off. "It's Reeves. Dr. Calvin Reeves."

There was a moment of stunned silence on the other end. "I've never heard of him. Sheila, just because you have a hunch—"

"I know how it sounds," she interrupted again, swerving around a slow-moving SUV. "But I've got evidence, Finn. He's connected to all the victims. He's part of Celestial Awakening. It all fits."

"Even if you're right, we can't just accuse someone without solid proof. We need to—"

"We need to find him before he kills again," Sheila snapped, no longer checking her frustration. "I'm done waiting, Finn. I'm done playing it safe while more women die. I'm going to Reeves' house, and I'm going to find the proof we need."

"Sheila, wait." Finn's voice was urgent now. "You can't go in there alone. It's not safe. If Reeves really is our killer—"

"Then I'll handle it," she said. "I need you to trust me on this, Finn. Can you do that?"

There was a long pause, filled only with the sound of Sheila's car engine and her own rapid breathing. Finally, Finn spoke. "Okay. But I'm coming, too. Don't do anything reckless before I get there, okay?"

"No promises," she said as she turned onto Reeves's street. "Just get here as quickly as you can." She ended the call before he could protest.

The house was a large Victorian, well-maintained and respectable-looking. Nothing on the outside hinted at the horrors Sheila suspected lay within. She parked across the street, her hand instinctively checking her weapon as she exited the car.

Approaching the house, Sheila's training kicked in. She observed the perfectly manicured lawn, the lights off inside, the absence of any vehicles in the driveway. It all suggested no one was home, but Sheila knew better than to trust appearances.

She rang the doorbell. "Police! Open up!"

No response. After a moment's hesitation, she tried the door handle. To her surprise, it turned easily.

"Dr. Reeves?" she called out as she entered, her voice echoing in the quiet house. "This is Deputy Stone. I need to ask you some questions."

Silence greeted her. Sheila moved cautiously through the house, her senses on high alert. The interior was immaculate, every surface polished, every item in its place. It reminded her of a showroom devoid of the lived-in feel of a real home.

In Reeves' study, Sheila found bookshelves lined with texts on psychology, religion, and astronomy. On his desk, a half-finished letter caught her eye. It was addressed to the medical board, expressing Reeves' intention to resign from his practice.

Sheila's heart raced. Was he planning to run?

As she continued her search, a nagging doubt began to creep in. What if she was wrong? What if this was just another dead end, and the real killer was still out there? The faces of the victims flashed through her mind, their eyes seeming to accuse her of failure.

Sheila shook her head, pushing the thoughts away. She couldn't afford to doubt herself now. She had to keep searching.

Finally, she came to a door she assumed led to the basement. Taking a deep breath, she opened it, revealing a set of stairs descending into darkness. Sheila flicked on her flashlight and began to descend, the old wood creaking under her feet.

The beam of her flashlight cut through the gloom, revealing a space that sent chills down her spine. Unlike the pristine rooms above, the basement was cluttered and chaotic. Tables were covered with strange symbols and diagrams. Shelves held jars of unidentifiable substances. And in the center of the room stood an altar, complete with candles and what looked disturbingly like bloodstains.

"My God," Sheila murmured, taking in the scene. This was it—proof that Reeves was their killer. But where was he?

And more importantly, where was his next victim?

A sudden creak from upstairs made Sheila freeze. Her hand instinctively went to her weapon as she listened intently. Another creak, followed by the sound of footsteps.

Someone was in the house.

Sheila's heart raced as she quietly made her way back up the basement stairs. She'd left the door slightly ajar when she came down, and now she peered through the crack, trying to catch a glimpse of the intruder.

A shadow moved across the hallway. Sheila held her breath, her fingers tightening on her gun. The footsteps grew closer. Just as she was about to burst out and confront the unknown person, a familiar voice called out softly.

"Sheila? You in here?"

Relief washed over her. "Finn," she whispered, pushing the door open. "I'm here."

Finn appeared in the hallway, his own weapon drawn. He lowered it with a sigh. "I take it you didn't find him."

"No luck so far."

"Well, I've got bad news, too. Just got a report about a missing woman. Megan Philips. Apparently, she was taken outside some kind of seminar—witnesses saw a man grab her and put her in his trunk."

"Did they get a license plate?"

Finn shook his head grimly. "No, not much of a description, either. The kidnapping was witnessed by a couple of middle schoolers on bikes. They said the man was tall and wore dark clothing, but that's about it."

"Well, at least she's still alive," Sheila murmured. "Or was."

"Oh, and one other thing. This seminar? It was being held at a community center, the same one where Reeves teaches."

Sheila cursed under her breath. "I knew it. He's our guy."

"Now we just have to find him," Finn said. He gestured at the open basement door behind Sheila. "Find anything interesting?"

Sheila nodded. "Come on, I'll show you."

She led Finn down the steps. As his flashlight beam joined hers in illuminating the basement, she heard his sharp intake of breath.

"Shit," Finn muttered, taking in the altar and the strange symbols covering the walls. "He's the Coldwater Confessor, alright."

Sheila nodded grimly. "But he's not here. And neither is Megan."

They made their way back upstairs, both lost in thought. In the kitchen, Finn leaned against the counter, running a hand through his hair. "Okay, let's think this through. If Reeves isn't here, where would he go? Where would he take Megan?"

Sheila paced the room. "He needs somewhere isolated, somewhere he won't be disturbed. But it also has to have some significance to him, to his twisted beliefs."

"What about going back to the community center?" Finn suggested. "That's where his group meets."

Sheila shook her head. "Too public. Even at night, there's a risk of someone walking in." She paused, a thought striking her. "Wait a minute. Reeves' wife—she was killed by lightning."

Finn studied her with a thoughtful frown. "You think that's connected to all this?"

"It has to be," Sheila said, her excitement growing. "That's probably what set him off, what made him start believing all this cosmic nonsense in the first place. We need to find out where it happened."

They began searching the house again, this time looking for any information about Helen Reeves' death. In Dr. Reeves' study, Sheila rifled through drawers while Finn scanned the bookshelves.

"Sheila," Finn called out suddenly. "Look at this."

He was holding a framed photo. It showed a younger Dr. Reeves with his arm around a smiling woman—presumably Helen. They were standing in front of a small cabin, trees visible in the background.

"Turn it over," Sheila said.

Finn flipped the frame, revealing a handwritten note on the back: 'Our last happy moment. Helen's Hideaway, Bear Creek Trail.'

"Bear Creek Trail," Sheila repeated, her pulse quickening. "That's up in the mountains, isn't it? There are a bunch of old cabins up there."

Finn was already pulling out his phone, searching for more information. "Yeah, it's about a fifteen-minute drive from here—ten if we're quick. Pretty isolated, especially this time of year."

Sheila's eyes lit up with determination. "That's got to be it. It's the perfect place for his 'cleansing ritual' or whatever he calls it."

As Finn called for backup, Sheila's gaze was drawn back to the photo. The smiling couple looked so normal, so happy. How had Dr. Reeves gone from that man to the monster they were now chasing?

She shook her head, pushing the thought aside. It didn't matter now. What mattered was stopping him before he could claim another victim.

"Backup's on the way," Finn said, pocketing his phone. "They'll meet us there."

Sheila nodded, already heading for the door. "Let's go. We can't wait for them to arrive."

As they rushed to their car, the sun had fully set, plunging Coldwater into darkness. Sheila couldn't shake the feeling that they were running out of time. Somewhere out there, in a cabin in the woods, an innocent woman's life hung in the balance.

And Dr. Calvin Reeves, the man they now knew as the Coldwater Confessor, was preparing for his final act of 'salvation.'

CHAPTER THIRTY

Megan's heart pounded in her chest as she watched Dr. Reeves raise the candlestick, its polished surface gleaming in the dim light. This couldn't be happening.

How had she gone from attending a community seminar to being tied up in a cabin, about to be murdered by a man she'd thought was there to help people?

She squeezed her eyes shut, bracing for the impact. But it never came.

"Open your eyes, Megan," Dr. Reeves said softly. "I want you to understand why this is necessary."

Trembling, Megan forced her eyes open. Dr. Reeves stood before her, candlestick still raised, a look of eerie calm on his face.

"Why are you doing this?" she asked.

Dr. Reeves smiled. It was a cold, unsettling expression. "Because you're lost, Megan. Like so many others. But through your sacrifice, you'll help bring about a new age of enlightenment."

Megan sensed he had more to say, so she waited, giving him plenty of space to speak.

"Do you know how many people live their lives in darkness, never realizing their true potential?" he asked. "I'm offering them a chance at redemption."

Megan's mind raced, searching for a way out. She needed to keep him talking, to buy herself more time. "But...but killing people? How does that help anyone?"

Dr. Reeves chuckled. "Oh, Megan. Death is just a transition. These souls, your soul, will serve a higher purpose."

"Higher purpose? What do you mean? Please help me understand."

He opened his mouth to speak, then closed it again. His smile fell away, and he narrowed his eyes. "You're stalling for time," he said. "What, you think someone's going to save you? You think help is on the way?"

She said nothing.

"Oh, Megan," he said. "I offered to help you, to show you the way, and you turned me down. You really think you're going to get a second chance?"

He raised the candlestick once more. This was it. Megan closed her eyes again, silently praying for a miracle.

Suddenly, a beam of light cut across the windows—headlights? Was someone here?

"It seems we may have company," Dr. Reeves muttered, lowering the candlestick. "How inconsiderate of them to interrupt our sacred moment."

As he moved toward the window, peering out into the darkness, Megan's mind raced. This might be her only chance. She had to do something, anything, to try and escape.

Her wrists burned where the ropes bit into her skin, but she forced herself to focus. Slowly, carefully, she began to rotate her hands, testing the bonds. They were tight, but not impossibly so. If she could just create a little slack...

Dr. Reeves was still at the window, muttering to himself about cosmic signs and divine intervention. Megan tuned him out, concentrating on the small movements of her hands. She could feel the ropes starting to loosen, just a fraction.

Emboldened, she increased her efforts, ignoring the pain as the rough fibers scraped against her skin. A bead of sweat trickled down her forehead, but she didn't dare move to wipe it away.

Just when she thought her wrists might give out, she felt it—a sudden give in the ropes. Her right hand slipped free.

Megan's heart leapt, but she forced herself to remain still. Dr. Reeves was still by the window, but he could turn around at any moment. She had to time this perfectly.

With agonizing slowness, she began working on the ropes binding her left hand. It was easier now that she had one hand free, but still painfully slow. She could hear Dr. Reeves moving around the room, muttering about preparing for unexpected guests.

Finally, her left hand came free. Megan allowed herself a small breath of relief, but she knew she wasn't out of danger yet. Her ankles were still bound to the chair legs.

She leaned down as much as she dared, her fingers fumbling with the knots. They were tight, seemingly impossible to undo. Panic started to rise in her throat. She was so close, but if she couldn't get her feet free—

"What do you think you're doing?"

Megan's blood ran cold. She looked up to see Dr. Reeves standing over her, his face a mask of fury. The candlestick was back in his hand, raised high.

In that moment, instinct took over. Megan threw herself sideways, chair and all. She hit the ground hard, the impact knocking the wind out of her. But the old chair couldn't take the force—it splintered, freeing her legs.

Dr. Reeves lunged for her, but Megan was already rolling. Ignoring the pain from her fall, she scrambled to her feet and ran for the door. She could hear him behind her, his breathing heavy, punctuated by mad ramblings about cleansing and cosmic justice.

Megan's hand closed around the doorknob. For one heart-stopping moment, she thought it might be locked. But then it turned, and she burst out into the cool night air.

The forest loomed before her, dark and foreboding. But it was her only chance. Without hesitation, Megan plunged into the trees.

Branches whipped at her face as she ran, her bare feet stumbling over roots and rocks. She could hear Dr. Reeves crashing through the underbrush behind her—close, too close. His voice carried through the night, alternating between coaxing and threatening.

"Come back, Megan! You don't understand—this is for your own good! Your soul needs cleansing!"

Megan didn't waste breath responding. She focused every ounce of her energy on running, on putting as much distance between herself and the madman behind her as possible.

She had no idea where she was going. The woods all looked the same in the darkness, and she had lost all sense of direction in her panic. But she knew she couldn't stop. Stopping meant death.

As she ran, her mind flashed back to earlier that evening. How normal everything had seemed. She had been leaving Dr. Reeves' seminar, her mind buzzing with thoughts about his talk on finding inner peace. He had approached her in the parking lot, all smiles and charm, asking if she'd like to discuss the seminar further over coffee.

She should have seen the signs. The way his eyes had gleamed with an unsettling intensity. The slight tremor in his hand as he'd gestured toward his car. But she'd been flattered by his attention, proud that the respected Dr. Reeves had singled her out.

Now, as she fled through the dark forest, the memory seemed like it belonged to another person.

A root caught her foot, sending her sprawling. Megan hit the ground hard, leaves and twigs scraping her exposed skin. For a moment, she lay there, the wind knocked out of her. Then she heard it—the sound of footsteps, getting closer.

Panic gave her a fresh surge of energy. Megan scrambled to her feet, ignoring the pain from her fall. She started running again, but she could tell she was slowing down. Her lungs burned, and her legs felt like lead.

"I can hear you, Megan!" Dr. Reeves called out, his voice far too close for comfort. "You can't escape your destiny. The stars themselves guide my hand!"

Megan's breath came in ragged gasps, and she could feel a stitch forming in her side. She couldn't keep this up much longer. She needed to hide, to find some way to throw Dr. Reeves off her trail. But where? In the darkness, every tree looked the same, every shadow a potential hiding spot—or a trap.

As she pushed through a dense patch of undergrowth, Megan's hand brushed against something solid. She paused, her heart pounding so loudly she was sure Dr. Reeves must be able to hear it. Carefully, she felt the object again. It was rough and vertical—a tree trunk, but larger than the others around it.

Megan ran her hands around the trunk. It was huge, far wider than she could encircle with her arms. An old-growth tree, ancient and imposing. And on one side, she felt it—a gap in the bark, an opening large enough for a person.

Without hesitation, Megan squeezed into the hollow tree. It was a tight fit, the rough interior scraping against her already battered skin, but she didn't care. All that mattered was that she was hidden.

She held her breath, listening. For a moment, all she could hear was the frantic beating of her own heart. Then, footsteps.

Slow, methodical, coming closer.

"Megan!" Dr. Reeves called, his tone both soothing and menacing. "I know you're close. I can sense your fear, your resistance to the cosmic truth. But you can't hide from destiny, Megan. You can't hide from me."

Inside her tree, Megan pressed a hand to her mouth, stifling the sobs that threatened to escape. She couldn't let him find her. She couldn't end up like the others—Laura, Sophie, Rachel, Emily. Their faces flashed through her mind, images she'd seen on the news. Had they been this terrified in their final moments?

The footsteps grew closer.

"You know, Megan," Dr. Reeves said, his voice terrifyingly close, "in many cultures, trees are seen as sacred. Conduits between the earthly realm and the cosmic beyond. How fitting it would be to find you embracing such a symbol."

Megan held her breath. Had he seen her? Was this the end?

But then the footsteps started moving again, growing fainter. He was moving away.

Megan wanted to sob with relief, but she didn't dare make a sound. She stayed frozen in place, barely breathing, for what felt like hours. Gradually, the sounds of the forest returned—the rustle of leaves, the distant hoot of an owl.

Still, she didn't move. What if it was a trick? What if Dr. Reeves was still out there, waiting for her to emerge?

But she couldn't stay in this tree forever. Her legs were cramping, and she was starting to feel lightheaded from fear and exhaustion. She had to do something.

Slowly, carefully, Megan began to ease herself out of the hollow tree. Every snapping twig, every rustle of leaves sounded impossibly loud to her ears. She emerged into the darkness, her eyes straining to see any sign of movement, any hint of danger.

Nothing. The forest was still.

Megan took a tentative step, then another. Which way should she go? She had no idea where she was, no concept of which direction might lead to safety. But she couldn't stay here.

Choosing a direction at random, Megan began to walk. Her movements were stiff at first, her muscles protesting after being cramped in the tree. But gradually, she picked up speed.

Just as Megan was starting to think she might be going in circles, she saw something through the trees—a faint glow. Could it be a road? Civilization?

Hope surged through her. Megan quickened her pace, moving toward the light. Yes—she could hear something now. Car engines. She was nearly there!

She burst through the treeline onto the shoulder of a road. In the distance, she could see headlights approaching. Megan waved her arms frantically, praying the driver would see her.

The car slowed, then pulled over. Megan nearly cried with relief.

But as the driver's door opened, a chill ran down her spine. A familiar silhouette stepped out, backlit by the headlights.

"I knew you'd find your way here eventually," Dr. Reeves said. "Are you ready to accept your destiny?"

CHAPTER THIRTY ONE

"CCSD!" Sheila called out as she and Finn reached the cabin. "Dr. Reeves, show yourself!"

Backup was already here. A local patrol had shown up first, but he'd followed orders and kept back, waiting for Sheila and Finn arrived. Now he stood outside his patrol car, hands on his hips.

"Keep an eye on the road!" Finn shouted to him as he and Sheila approached the cabin. "Make sure no one leaves!"

Sheila and Finn reached the cabin and paused. "This is your last warning!" she shouted. "Come on out!"

There was no answer. The two deputies exchanged a nod, and then Finn kicked the door open. They entered, guns drawn, ready for anything.

But the cabin was empty. Signs of a struggle were evident: an overturned chair, ropes discarded on the floor.

"We're too late," Finn muttered, holstering his weapon.

Sheila was about to respond when a distant sound caught her attention. "Wait, did you hear that?"

They rushed outside, straining their ears. There it was again: a faint shout carried on the wind.

"This way," Sheila said, plunging into the forest with Finn close behind.

Sheila moved as quickly as she dared through the dark woods, guided only by her flashlight and the intermittent sounds. Branches whipped at her face, and roots threatened to trip her at every step.

Suddenly, the trees thinned, and she found herself at the edge of a road. In the distance, Sheila could make out two figures illuminated by a car's headlights.

"There!" she said.

As they sprinted toward the scene, Sheila saw a man—Dr. Reeves, she presumed—lunge at a long-haired figure, presumably Megan. Without breaking stride, Sheila raised her gun.

"Drop the weapon!" she shouted, her voice ringing out in the night. "Police! Dr. Reeves, put your hands where I can see them!"

Reeves whirled around, surprise evident on his face. But it quickly morphed into an eerily calm smile. "Ah, the police. I should have known you'd find us eventually. You're just in time to witness the cleansing."

"The only thing you'll be witnessing is the inside of a jail cell," Sheila said, her gun trained on Reeves. "Now drop the weapon and step away from Ms. Philips."

"Do it!" Finn said.

For a moment, it seemed like Reeves might comply. He lowered the candlestick slightly, his eyes darting between Sheila and his captive. Then, with startling speed, he lunged at Megan.

Sheila fired, but Reeves was faster than she'd anticipated. The bullet grazed his arm, but it didn't stop him. He grabbed Megan, pulling her close and holding the candlestick across her throat with both hands.

"Drop your weapons," he said, his voice unnervingly calm. "Or I'll crush Miss Megan's larynx."

Sheila's mouth went dry. She couldn't risk Megan's life, but if she gave up her gun...

"Okay," she said slowly, crouching to place her gun on the ground.

"What are you doing?" Finn whispered.

"We have no choice," she whispered back. Then she turned her attention to Dr. Reeves again. "Let's talk about this, Dr. Reeves. You don't want to hurt Megan. That's not who you are."

Reeves laughed, a chilling sound. "You have no idea who I am, Deputy. I am an instrument of cosmic justice. The stars themselves guide my hand!"

"The stars didn't guide your hand when you killed Laura, or Sophie, or Rachel, or Emily," Sheila said, straightening up slowly. "That was all you, Calvin. You made those choices."

A flicker of uncertainty crossed Reeves' face. "No, you don't understand. They rejected the truth. They had to be cleansed."

"Cleansed?" Sheila took a cautious step forward. "Or punished? They rejected you, didn't they? Just like your wife did." It was a shot in the dark, but perhaps it would land.

Reeves' grip on Megan tightened, causing her to whimper. "Helen didn't reject me. She was taken. The lightning...it was a sign."

"A sign of what?" Sheila pressed, taking another small step. "That you should become a killer? That you should destroy lives instead of helping people like you used to?"

"I *am* helping people!" Reeves shouted, his calm facade cracking. "I'm saving their souls!"

"You're not saving anyone, Calvin," Sheila said softly. "You're just a man who couldn't handle loss. Who couldn't accept that sometimes, terrible things happen for no reason."

Reeves shook his head violently. "No, no, you're wrong. The cosmic plan…the divine justice..."

While Reeves was distracted, Megan suddenly drove her elbow back into his stomach. He doubled over, loosening his grip. Megan tore free, running toward Sheila.

Reeves recovered quickly, rage contorting his features. He raised the candlestick, charging at them both.

Sheila pushed Megan behind her, dropping into a defensive stance. As Reeves swung the candlestick, she ducked under his arm, driving her fist into his solar plexus. Reeves stumbled back, gasping for air.

But he wasn't done. With a roar of fury, he attacked again. Reeves swung the candlestick in a wide arc, the metal glinting in the car's headlights. Sheila ducked, feeling the rush of air as the makeshift weapon passed inches from her head. She spun, using her momentum to drive an elbow into Reeves' ribs.

He grunted but didn't slow down. His free hand shot out, grabbing a fistful of Sheila's jacket. She twisted, breaking his grip, and countered with a quick jab to his solar plexus. Reeves stumbled back, wheezing, but his eyes blazed with manic intensity.

Sheila bounced on the balls of her feet, fists raised, ready for his next move. Reeves feinted left, then lunged right, the candlestick whistling through the air. Sheila sidestepped, but not quite fast enough. The edge of the candlestick caught her shoulder, sending a jolt of pain down her arm.

She gritted her teeth, refusing to let the pain slow her down. As Reeves pulled back for another swing, Sheila saw an opening. She stepped in close, inside his guard, and drove her knee up into his midsection. Reeves doubled over, but as Sheila tried to back away, he wrapped his arms around her waist, tackling her to the ground.

They hit the asphalt hard, the impact knocking the wind out of Sheila. Reeves was on top of her, his weight pinning her down. The candlestick lay forgotten nearby as he wrapped his hands around her throat. Sheila clawed at his fingers, gasping for air. Her vision began to darken at the edges.

With a surge of desperate strength, Sheila bucked her hips, destabilizing Reeves' position. She managed to get one leg free and hooked it around his torso. Using the leverage, she rolled them over, reversing their positions.

Now on top, Sheila rained down blows, her fists connecting with Reeves' face and chest. But he seemed to feel no pain, his hands still reaching for her, eyes wild with rage and madness. It was almost like he wanted this—he wanted to be punished.

Disgusted, Sheila pushed off him and stood. Reeves scrambled to his feet, coughing, but before he could lunge at Sheila again, a shot rang out. Sheila turned to see Finn, his gun still pointed at the sky.

"It's over, Reeves," Finn said. "On the ground, now."

Reeves looked from Finn to Sheila, then to Megan. For a moment, Sheila thought he might try to run. But then, like a puppet with its strings cut, he collapsed to his knees.

"I was so close," he mumbled. "So close to completing the cleansing..."

As Finn moved in to handcuff Reeves, Sheila went to check on Megan. The young woman was shaking, tears streaming down her face.

"It's okay," Sheila said softly, putting an arm around her. "You're safe now. It's over."

In the distance, Sheila could hear sirens approaching. Backup was on its way. As she watched Finn lead Reeves to their car, a wave of relief washed over her. They had done it. They had caught the Coldwater Confessor.

But as she looked at Megan, still trembling beside her, Sheila knew the effects of Reeves' actions would linger long after he was behind bars. The healing process for Coldwater was just beginning.

And Sheila vowed to herself that she would be there every step of the way, helping her town recover from the nightmare it had endured. Because that's what she did. That's who she was.

A protector. A seeker of justice. A guardian of Coldwater.

And as the emergency vehicles, Sheila knew that whatever challenges lay ahead, she was ready to face them. For herself, for the victims, and for the town she had sworn to protect.

EPILOGUE

The morning sun cast a warm glow over Coldwater as Sheila stood on the steps of the police station, watching the last of the reporters drive away.

Well, that took forever, she thought, sighing.

The press conference had been grueling, but necessary. The town needed to know that the nightmare was over, that the Coldwater Confessor had been caught.

Sheila felt a presence beside her and turned to see Finn, two steaming cups of coffee in his hands. He offered her one, which she accepted gratefully.

"How are you holding up?" he asked, his voice gentle.

Sheila took a sip of coffee before answering. "Honestly? I'm not sure. It doesn't feel real yet."

They stood in companionable silence for a moment, watching the town slowly come to life. After days of fear and suspicion, people were finally emerging from their homes, tentatively reclaiming their streets and routines.

"You know," Finn said, breaking the silence, "I've been thinking about what Dawson said. About the department looking for a permanent replacement for Natalie."

Sheila tensed slightly at the mention of her sister's name. "What about it?"

Finn turned to face her, his expression serious. "I think you should go for it, Sheila. You'd make an amazing sheriff."

Sheila shook her head, a rueful smile on her face. "I'm not Natalie, Finn. I never have been."

"No, you're not," Finn agreed. "You're Sheila. And that's more than good enough. Look at how you handled this case. Your instincts, your determination—they're exactly what this town needs."

Sheila felt a lump forming in her throat. She turned away, blinking back unexpected tears. "I don't know if I'm ready for that kind of responsibility."

Finn's hand on her shoulder was warm and reassuring. "I think you are. And I think Natalie would be proud of you."

At the mention of her sister, the dam broke. Sheila felt the tears she'd been holding back for so long finally spill over. Finn pulled her into a hug, and she let herself be held, her body shaking with silent sobs.

When she finally pulled away, wiping her eyes, she saw understanding in Finn's gaze. No judgment, no pity. Just acceptance and something else...something that made her heart race.

"No pressure," Finn added. "It's your life. I guess…I guess I just want you to know that I believe in you."

Sheila smiled and leaned in, their lips meeting in a kiss that felt like coming home.

When they finally parted, Sheila felt a newfound sense of purpose. "Maybe you're right," she said. "Maybe I am ready to be sheriff. But only if I have you by my side."

Finn grinned. "Always, partner. Always. Now…" He placed both hands on her shoulders and stared into her eyes. "I want you to do something very important for me."

"Okay…" Sheila said, drawing the word out.

"I want you to go home, shower, and get some sleep. You need it."

Sheila grunted. "Okay, but don't think this means you can give me orders. I might be your boss soon, after all."

Finn rolled his eyes. "Oh, boy. It's already getting to your head."

She smiled innocently. "It's your fault for suggesting the idea."

***

Sheila stepped out of the shower, wrapping herself in a fluffy towel. The hot water had washed away some of the physical exhaustion, but it had done nothing to slow her feverish thoughts.

Finn's words echoed in her head as she dried her hair: *You'd make an amazing sheriff.*

She stared at her reflection in the foggy mirror. Could she really do it? Take on the responsibility of leading the entire department? The thought was both exhilarating and terrifying.

As she walked into her bedroom, her eyes fell on a framed photo of Natalie on her dresser. Her sister's smile, frozen in time, seemed to offer encouragement. Sheila picked up the frame, running her thumb over the glass.

"What would you think, Nat?" she whispered. "Am I crazy for even considering this?"

A muffled thud from down the hall interrupted her thoughts. Sheila tensed for a moment before remembering: Star. The teenager she'd taken in was probably just rummaging around in her room.

Sheila sighed, setting down the photo. Star was another responsibility, another challenge she'd taken on. The girl had been through so much, and connecting with her was proving to be difficult. But Sheila was determined to help her, to give her the stability and support she desperately needed.

As she got dressed, Sheila's mind drifted to Finn again. Their relationship was progressing so quickly, and she felt an ease and familiarity with him that she hadn't expected to find with anyone. This was wonderful, but it also complicated things. If she became sheriff, would their personal relationship affect their professional one?

Sheila shook her head, trying to clear her thoughts. She was overthinking everything. Right now, she needed sleep. She could worry about the future tomorrow.

Just as she was about to climb into bed, a soft knock came at her door.

"Sheila?" Star's voice was hesitant. "Are you awake?"

Sheila opened the door to find the teenager standing there, looking uncomfortable. "What's up, Star? Everything okay?"

Star shrugged, not meeting Sheila's eyes. "I just...I heard about what happened. With the Coldwater Confessor. I wanted to make sure you were alright."

Sheila felt a warmth in her chest. This was the first time Star had reached out like this. "I'm okay, Star. Thank you for asking. It's been a long couple of days, but it's over now."

Star nodded, fidgeting with the hem of her shirt. "That's good. I'm glad you're safe." She paused, then added quickly, "Goodnight," before darting back to her room.

Sheila watched her go, a small smile on her face. It wasn't much, but it was progress.

Finally settling into bed, Sheila felt the exhaustion of the past few days washing over her. Her eyelids grew heavy, and she was just about to drift off when her phone buzzed on the nightstand.

Groaning, she reached for it, squinting at the bright screen. It was a message from dispatch, marked urgent. The message was brief, but it made Sheila's blood run cold:

Vehicle matching description of Eddie Mills' car spotted at gas station off Highway 50. Driver fled when approached by highway patrol. Matches Mills' description. Heading east toward the state line.

Sleep forgotten, Sheila sat up. Eddie Mills, the man she believed responsible for her mother's unsolved murder, was within reach. After years of dead ends and false leads, this could be her chance to finally bring him to justice.

Without hesitation, Sheila got dressed and grabbed her keys and badge. As she headed for the door, she paused, looking back toward Star's room. She couldn't leave without saying anything.

Quickly, she scribbled a note: *Star, had to go out for work. There's food in the fridge. Call if you need anything. — Sheila*

She slipped the note under Star's door, then rushed out to her car. As she pulled out of the driveway, her phone buzzed again. It was Finn.

Just got the alert about Mills. Want me to meet you at the station?

Sheila paused, her hand hovering over the phone. She thought about Finn, about their conversation earlier. About the future they'd talked about building together. She couldn't betray that now.

Yes, she wrote back. *Thanks, Finn.*

As she merged onto the highway, Sheila felt a familiar determination settle over her. The Coldwater Confessor case might be closed, but her own personal mission was far from over.

"I'm coming for you, Eddie," she muttered as she pressed down on the accelerator. "It's time to finish this."

As Sheila's car disappeared into the night, the quiet streets of Coldwater held no hint of the storm brewing on the horizon. The town had weathered one nightmare, but for Sheila Stone, a new chapter was just beginning.

And this time, it was personal.

NOW AVAILABLE!

SILENT NEIGHBOR
(A Sheila Stone Suspense Thriller—Book Nine)

With a career-ending injury, Olympic kickboxer Sheila Stone is forced back to her small hometown, where her older sister, the local sheriff, offers her a spot on the local police force.

When adrenaline junkies are found suspended from Utah's treacherous cliffs, Sheila Stone must navigate the perilous heights and decode the killer's message, punishing those who dare to conquer nature for vanity—before she becomes the next trophy.

"A masterpiece of thriller and mystery."
—Books and Movie Reviews, Roberto Mattos (re Once Gone)

SILENT NEIGHBOR (A Sheila Stone Suspense Thriller—Book 9) is the ninth book in a long-anticipated new series by #1 bestseller and USA Today bestselling author Blake Pierce, whose bestseller *The Perfect Wife* (a free download) has received over 20,000 five star reviews.

With her Olympic dreams crumbled, Sheila, 28, struggles to find her place back home. She is surrounded by reminders of what could have been, stuck inside the shadow of her older sister: the golden child, the respected sheriff. But when her sister persuades her to join the local police force, Sheila's life and career start anew.

As she hunts serial killers, Sheila notices clues that others miss and offers a perspective that no one else has. She realizes she has a talent outside of fighting, and that she has a chance to embrace a new life in Salt Lake—a life outside the ring.

This is a different kind of ring, though. Sheila quickly realizes that to survive, she will need more than just her strength—she'll need a brilliance to match that of even the most diabolical killer….
Can Sheila win this match? Or will she finally lose it all?

A page-turning and harrowing suspense thriller featuring a brilliant and tortured protagonist, the SHEILA STONE series is a riveting mystery, packed with suspense, twists and turns, revelations, and driven by a breakneck pace that will keep you flipping pages late into the night.

Future books in the series are also available.

"An edge of your seat thriller in a new series that keeps you turning pages! ...So many twists, turns and red herrings… I can't wait to see what happens next."
—Reader review (Her Last Wish)

"A strong, complex story about two FBI agents trying to stop a serial killer. If you want an author to capture your attention and have you guessing, yet trying to put the pieces together, Pierce is your author!"
—Reader review (Her Last Wish)

"A typical Blake Pierce twisting, turning, roller coaster ride suspense thriller. Will have you turning the pages to the last sentence of the last chapter!!!"
—Reader review (City of Prey)

"Right from the start we have an unusual protagonist that I haven't seen done in this genre before. The action is nonstop… A very atmospheric novel that will keep you turning pages well into the wee hours."
—Reader review (City of Prey)

"Everything that I look for in a book… a great plot, interesting characters, and grabs your interest right away. The book moves along at a breakneck pace and stays that way until the end. Now on go I to book two!"
—Reader review (Girl, Alone)

"Exciting, heart pounding, edge of your seat book… a must read for mystery and suspense readers!"
—Reader review (Girl, Alone)

Blake Pierce

Blake Pierce is the USA Today bestselling author of the RILEY PAGE mystery series, which includes seventeen books. Blake Pierce is also the author of the MACKENZIE WHITE mystery series, comprising fourteen books; of the AVERY BLACK mystery series, comprising six books; of the KERI LOCKE mystery series, comprising five books; of the MAKING OF RILEY PAIGE mystery series, comprising six books; of the KATE WISE mystery series, comprising seven books; of the CHLOE FINE psychological suspense mystery, comprising six books; of the JESSIE HUNT psychological suspense thriller series, comprising thirty-eight books (and counting); of the AU PAIR psychological suspense thriller series, comprising three books; of the ZOE PRIME mystery series, comprising six books; of the ADELE SHARP mystery series, comprising sixteen books, of the EUROPEAN VOYAGE cozy mystery series, comprising six books; of the LAURA FROST FBI suspense thriller, comprising eleven books; of the ELLA DARK FBI suspense thriller, comprising twenty-five books (and counting); of the A YEAR IN EUROPE cozy mystery series, comprising nine books, of the AVA GOLD mystery series, comprising six books; of the RACHEL GIFT mystery series, comprising fifteen books; of the VALERIE LAW mystery series, comprising nine books; of the PAIGE KING mystery series, comprising eight books; of the MAY MOORE mystery series, comprising eleven books; of the CORA SHIELDS mystery series, comprising eight books; of the NICKY LYONS mystery series, comprising eight books, of the CAMI LARK mystery series, comprising ten books; of the AMBER YOUNG mystery series, comprising eight books; of the DAISY FORTUNE mystery series, comprising five books; of the FIONA RED mystery series, comprising thirteen books; of the FAITH BOLD mystery series, comprising twenty books (and counting); of the JULIETTE HART mystery series, comprising five books; of the MORGAN CROSS mystery series, comprising thirteen books; of the FINN WRIGHT mystery series, comprising seven books; of the SHEILA STONE suspense thriller series, comprising ten books; of the RACHEL BLACKWOOD suspense thriller series, comprising eight books; of the THE GOVERNESS psychological suspense thriller series, comprising nine books (and counting); and of the new JENNA GRAVES mystery series, comprising eight books (and counting).

An avid reader and lifelong fan of the mystery and thriller genres, Blake loves to hear from you, so please feel free to visit www.blakepierceauthor.com to learn more and stay in touch.

BOOKS BY BLAKE PIERCE

JENNA GRAVES SUSPENSE THRILLER

IN HER SIGHTS (Book #1)
IN HER MIND (Book #2)
IN HER GRASP (Book #3)
IN HER SHADOW (Book #4)
IN HER PRAYERS (Book #5)
IN HER BED (Book #6)
IN HER DREAMS (Book #7)
IN HER FEARS (Book #8)

THE GOVERNESS PSYCHOLOGICAL SUSPENSE

ONE LAST LIE (Book #1)
ONE LAST SMILE (Book #2)
ONE LAST BREATH (Book #3)
ONE LAST GOODBYE (Book #4)
ONE LAST SECRET (Book #5)
ONE LAST WHISPER (Book #6)
ONE LAST REGRET (Book #7)
ONE LAST NIGHT (Book #8)
ONE LAST STEP (Book #9)

RACHEL BLACKWOOD SUSPENSE THRILLER

NOT THIS WAY (Book #1)
NOT THIS TIME (Book #2)
NOT THIS CLOSE (Book #3)
NOT THIS ROAD (Book #4)
NOT THIS LATE (Book #5)
NOT THIS NIGHT (Book #6)
NOT THIS PLACE (Book #7)
NOT THIS SOON (Book #8)

SHEILA STONE SUSPENSE THRILLER

SILENT GIRL (Book #1)
SILENT TRAIL (Book #2)
SILENT NIGHT (Book #3)

SILENT HOUSE (Book #4)
SILENT SCREAM (Book #5)
SILENT PREY (Book #6)
SILENT RITUAL (Book #7)
SILENT PRAYER (Book #8)
SILENT NEIGHBOR (Book #9)
SILENT SMILE (Book #10)

FINN WRIGHT MYSTERY SERIES
WHEN YOU'RE MINE (Book #1)
WHEN YOU'RE SAFE (Book #2)
WHEN YOU'RE CLOSE (Book #3)
WHEN YOU'RE SLEEPING (Book #4)
WHEN YOU'RE SANE (Book #5)
WHEN YOU'RE SILENT (Book #6)
WHEN YOU'RE GONE (Book #7)

MORGAN CROSS MYSTERY SERIES
FOR YOU (Book #1)
FOR RAGE (Book #2)
FOR LUST (Book #3)
FOR WRATH (Book #4)
FOREVER (Book #5)
FOR US (Book #6)
FOR NOW (Book #7)
FOR ONCE (Book #8)
FOR ETERNITY (Book #9)
FORLORN (Book #10)
FOR SILENCE (Book #11)
FORBIDDEN (Book #12)
FOR FEAR (Book #13)
FORSAKEN (Book #14)

JULIETTE HART MYSTERY SERIES
NOTHING TO FEAR (Book #1)
NOTHING THERE (Book #2)
NOTHING WATCHING (Book #3)
NOTHING HIDING (Book #4)
NOTHING LEFT (Book #5)

FAITH BOLD MYSTERY SERIES

SO LONG (Book #1)
SO COLD (Book #2)
SO SCARED (Book #3)
SO NORMAL (Book #4)
SO FAR GONE (Book #5)
SO LOST (Book #6)
SO ALONE (Book #7)
SO FORGOTTEN (Book #8)
SO INSANE (Book #9)
SO SMITTEN (Book #10)
SO SIMPLE (Book #11)
SO BROKEN (Book #12)
SO CRUEL (Book #13)
SO HAUNTED (Book #14)
SO SILENT (Book #15)
SO BLEAK (Book #16)
SO HOLLOW (Book #17)
SO DARK (Book #18)
SO TWISTED (Book #19)
SO WICKED (Book #20)

FIONA RED MYSTERY SERIES

LET HER GO (Book #1)
LET HER BE (Book #2)
LET HER HOPE (Book #3)
LET HER WISH (Book #4)
LET HER LIVE (Book #5)
LET HER RUN (Book #6)
LET HER HIDE (Book #7)
LET HER BELIEVE (Book #8)
LET HER FORGET (Book #9)
LET HER TRY (Book #10)
LET HER PLAY (Book #11)
LET HER VANISH (Book #12)
LET HER FADE (Book #13)

DAISY FORTUNE MYSTERY SERIES

NEED YOU (Book #1)
CLAIM YOU (Book #2)

CRAVE YOU (Book #3)
CHOOSE YOU (Book #4)
CHASE YOU (Book #5)

AMBER YOUNG MYSTERY SERIES
ABSENT PITY (Book #1)
ABSENT REMORSE (Book #2)
ABSENT FEELING (Book #3)
ABSENT MERCY (Book #4)
ABSENT REASON (Book #5)
ABSENT SANITY (Book #6)
ABSENT LIFE (Book #7)
ABSENT HUMANITY (Book #8)

CAMI LARK MYSTERY SERIES
JUST ME (Book #1)
JUST OUTSIDE (Book #2)
JUST RIGHT (Book #3)
JUST FORGET (Book #4)
JUST ONCE (Book #5)
JUST HIDE (Book #6)
JUST NOW (Book #7)
JUST HOPE (Book #8)
JUST LEAVE (Book #9)
JUST TONIGHT (Book #10)

NICKY LYONS MYSTERY SERIES
ALL MINE (Book #1)
ALL HIS (Book #2)
ALL HE SEES (Book #3)
ALL ALONE (Book #4)
ALL FOR ONE (Book #5)
ALL HE TAKES (Book #6)
ALL FOR ME (Book #7)
ALL IN (Book #8)

CORA SHIELDS MYSTERY SERIES
UNDONE (Book #1)
UNWANTED (Book #2)
UNHINGED (Book #3)

UNSAID (Book #4)
UNGLUED (Book #5)
UNSTABLE (Book #6)
UNKNOWN (Book #7)
UNAWARE (Book #8)

MAY MOORE SUSPENSE THRILLER
NEVER RUN (Book #1)
NEVER TELL (Book #2)
NEVER LIVE (Book #3)
NEVER HIDE (Book #4)
NEVER FORGIVE (Book #5)
NEVER AGAIN (Book #6)
NEVER LOOK BACK (Book #7)
NEVER FORGET (Book #8)
NEVER LET GO (Book #9)
NEVER PRETEND (Book #10)
NEVER HESITATE (Book #11)

PAIGE KING MYSTERY SERIES
THE GIRL HE PINED (Book #1)
THE GIRL HE CHOSE (Book #2)
THE GIRL HE TOOK (Book #3)
THE GIRL HE WISHED (Book #4)
THE GIRL HE CROWNED (Book #5)
THE GIRL HE WATCHED (Book #6)
THE GIRL HE WANTED (Book #7)
THE GIRL HE CLAIMED (Book #8)

VALERIE LAW MYSTERY SERIES
NO MERCY (Book #1)
NO PITY (Book #2)
NO FEAR (Book #3)
NO SLEEP (Book #4)
NO QUARTER (Book #5)
NO CHANCE (Book #6)
NO REFUGE (Book #7)
NO GRACE (Book #8)
NO ESCAPE (Book #9)

RACHEL GIFT MYSTERY SERIES
HER LAST WISH (Book #1)
HER LAST CHANCE (Book #2)
HER LAST HOPE (Book #3)
HER LAST FEAR (Book #4)
HER LAST CHOICE (Book #5)
HER LAST BREATH (Book #6)
HER LAST MISTAKE (Book #7)
HER LAST DESIRE (Book #8)
HER LAST REGRET (Book #9)
HER LAST HOUR (Book #10)
HER LAST SHOT (Book #11)
HER LAST PRAYER (Book #12)
HER LAST LIE (Book #13)
HER LAST WHISPER (Book #14)
HER LAST SECRET (Book #15)

AVA GOLD MYSTERY SERIES
CITY OF PREY (Book #1)
CITY OF FEAR (Book #2)
CITY OF BONES (Book #3)
CITY OF GHOSTS (Book #4)
CITY OF DEATH (Book #5)
CITY OF VICE (Book #6)

A YEAR IN EUROPE
A MURDER IN PARIS (Book #1)
DEATH IN FLORENCE (Book #2)
VENGEANCE IN VIENNA (Book #3)
A FATALITY IN SPAIN (Book #4)

ELLA DARK FBI SUSPENSE THRILLER
GIRL, ALONE (Book #1)
GIRL, TAKEN (Book #2)
GIRL, HUNTED (Book #3)
GIRL, SILENCED (Book #4)
GIRL, VANISHED (Book 5)
GIRL ERASED (Book #6)
GIRL, FORSAKEN (Book #7)
GIRL, TRAPPED (Book #8)

GIRL, EXPENDABLE (Book #9)
GIRL, ESCAPED (Book #10)
GIRL, HIS (Book #11)
GIRL, LURED (Book #12)
GIRL, MISSING (Book #13)
GIRL, UNKNOWN (Book #14)
GIRL, DECEIVED (Book #15)
GIRL, FORLORN (Book #16)
GIRL, REMADE (Book #17)
GIRL, BETRAYED (Book #18)
GIRL, BOUND (Book #19)
GIRL, REFORMED (Book #20)
GIRL, REBORN (Book #21)
GIRL, HAUNTED (Book #22)
GIRL, UNSEEN (Book #23)
GIRL, SOUGHT (Book #24)
GIRL, ACCUSED (Book #25)

LAURA FROST FBI SUSPENSE THRILLER
ALREADY GONE (Book #1)
ALREADY SEEN (Book #2)
ALREADY TRAPPED (Book #3)
ALREADY MISSING (Book #4)
ALREADY DEAD (Book #5)
ALREADY TAKEN (Book #6)
ALREADY CHOSEN (Book #7)
ALREADY LOST (Book #8)
ALREADY HIS (Book #9)
ALREADY LURED (Book #10)
ALREADY COLD (Book #11)

EUROPEAN VOYAGE COZY MYSTERY SERIES
MURDER (AND BAKLAVA) (Book #1)
DEATH (AND APPLE STRUDEL) (Book #2)
CRIME (AND LAGER) (Book #3)
MISFORTUNE (AND GOUDA) (Book #4)
CALAMITY (AND A DANISH) (Book #5)
MAYHEM (AND HERRING) (Book #6)

ADELE SHARP MYSTERY SERIES

LEFT TO DIE (Book #1)
LEFT TO RUN (Book #2)
LEFT TO HIDE (Book #3)
LEFT TO KILL (Book #4)
LEFT TO MURDER (Book #5)
LEFT TO ENVY (Book #6)
LEFT TO LAPSE (Book #7)
LEFT TO VANISH (Book #8)
LEFT TO HUNT (Book #9)
LEFT TO FEAR (Book #10)
LEFT TO PREY (Book #11)
LEFT TO LURE (Book #12)
LEFT TO CRAVE (Book #13)
LEFT TO LOATHE (Book #14)
LEFT TO HARM (Book #15)
LEFT TO RUIN (Book #16)

THE AU PAIR SERIES
ALMOST GONE (Book#1)
ALMOST LOST (Book #2)
ALMOST DEAD (Book #3)

ZOE PRIME MYSTERY SERIES
FACE OF DEATH (Book#1)
FACE OF MURDER (Book #2)
FACE OF FEAR (Book #3)
FACE OF MADNESS (Book #4)
FACE OF FURY (Book #5)
FACE OF DARKNESS (Book #6)

A JESSIE HUNT PSYCHOLOGICAL SUSPENSE SERIES
THE PERFECT WIFE (Book #1)
THE PERFECT BLOCK (Book #2)
THE PERFECT HOUSE (Book #3)
THE PERFECT SMILE (Book #4)
THE PERFECT LIE (Book #5)
THE PERFECT LOOK (Book #6)
THE PERFECT AFFAIR (Book #7)
THE PERFECT ALIBI (Book #8)
THE PERFECT NEIGHBOR (Book #9)

THE PERFECT DISGUISE (Book #10)
THE PERFECT SECRET (Book #11)
THE PERFECT FAÇADE (Book #12)
THE PERFECT IMPRESSION (Book #13)
THE PERFECT DECEIT (Book #14)
THE PERFECT MISTRESS (Book #15)
THE PERFECT IMAGE (Book #16)
THE PERFECT VEIL (Book #17)
THE PERFECT INDISCRETION (Book #18)
THE PERFECT RUMOR (Book #19)
THE PERFECT COUPLE (Book #20)
THE PERFECT MURDER (Book #21)
THE PERFECT HUSBAND (Book #22)
THE PERFECT SCANDAL (Book #23)
THE PERFECT MASK (Book #24)
THE PERFECT RUSE (Book #25)
THE PERFECT VENEER (Book #26)
THE PERFECT PEOPLE (Book #27)
THE PERFECT WITNESS (Book #28)
THE PERFECT APPEARANCE (Book #29)
THE PERFECT TRAP (Book #30)
THE PERFECT EXPRESSION (Book #31)
THE PERFECT ACCOMPLICE (Book #32)
THE PERFECT SHOW (Book #33)
THE PERFECT POISE (Book #34)
THE PERFECT CROWD (Book #35)
THE PERFECT CRIME (Book #36)
THE PERFECT PREY (Book #37)
THE PERFECT BETRAYAL (Book #38)

CHLOE FINE PSYCHOLOGICAL SUSPENSE SERIES

NEXT DOOR (Book #1)
A NEIGHBOR'S LIE (Book #2)
CUL DE SAC (Book #3)
SILENT NEIGHBOR (Book #4)
HOMECOMING (Book #5)
TINTED WINDOWS (Book #6)

KATE WISE MYSTERY SERIES

IF SHE KNEW (Book #1)

IF SHE SAW (Book #2)
IF SHE RAN (Book #3)
IF SHE HID (Book #4)
IF SHE FLED (Book #5)
IF SHE FEARED (Book #6)
IF SHE HEARD (Book #7)

THE MAKING OF RILEY PAIGE SERIES

WATCHING (Book #1)
WAITING (Book #2)
LURING (Book #3)
TAKING (Book #4)
STALKING (Book #5)
KILLING (Book #6)

RILEY PAIGE MYSTERY SERIES

ONCE GONE (Book #1)
ONCE TAKEN (Book #2)
ONCE CRAVED (Book #3)
ONCE LURED (Book #4)
ONCE HUNTED (Book #5)
ONCE PINED (Book #6)
ONCE FORSAKEN (Book #7)
ONCE COLD (Book #8)
ONCE STALKED (Book #9)
ONCE LOST (Book #10)
ONCE BURIED (Book #11)
ONCE BOUND (Book #12)
ONCE TRAPPED (Book #13)
ONCE DORMANT (Book #14)
ONCE SHUNNED (Book #15)
ONCE MISSED (Book #16)
ONCE CHOSEN (Book #17)

MACKENZIE WHITE MYSTERY SERIES

BEFORE HE KILLS (Book #1)
BEFORE HE SEES (Book #2)
BEFORE HE COVETS (Book #3)
BEFORE HE TAKES (Book #4)
BEFORE HE NEEDS (Book #5)

BEFORE HE FEELS (Book #6)
BEFORE HE SINS (Book #7)
BEFORE HE HUNTS (Book #8)
BEFORE HE PREYS (Book #9)
BEFORE HE LONGS (Book #10)
BEFORE HE LAPSES (Book #11)
BEFORE HE ENVIES (Book #12)
BEFORE HE STALKS (Book #13)
BEFORE HE HARMS (Book #14)

AVERY BLACK MYSTERY SERIES
CAUSE TO KILL (Book #1)
CAUSE TO RUN (Book #2)
CAUSE TO HIDE (Book #3)
CAUSE TO FEAR (Book #4)
CAUSE TO SAVE (Book #5)
CAUSE TO DREAD (Book #6)

KERI LOCKE MYSTERY SERIES
A TRACE OF DEATH (Book #1)
A TRACE OF MURDER (Book #2)
A TRACE OF VICE (Book #3)
A TRACE OF CRIME (Book #4)
A TRACE OF HOPE (Book #5)

Manufactured by Amazon.ca
Bolton, ON

40998871R00111